PAMELA SARGENT

EYE OF THE COMET

1 8 1 7

HARPER & ROW, PUBLISHERS

Cambridge, Philadelphia, San Francisco, London, Mexico City, São Paulo, Sydney

NEW YORK

Library of Congress Cataloging in Publication Data
Sargent, Pamela.
  Eye of the comet.

  Summary: a young girl, living on a comet world, is
assigned the task of returning to her home planet Earth
to act as a bridge between the two very different
cultures.
  [1. Science fiction] I. Title.
PZ7.S2472Ey 1984   [Fic]   83-47696
ISBN 0-06-025196-4
ISBN 0-06-025197-2 (lib. bdg.)

For Kathryn

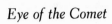
Eye of the Comet

1

Lydee's head ached. Stretching out on her bed, she lifted a hand to her brow and then remembered. She no longer had to wear a circlet. Briefly, she touched her forehead near the spot where her implant had been inserted.

Through the tiny, implanted link, she would now be able to communicate with Homesmind whenever she wished, and with others as well. The link could be closed if she did not wish to speak, but she could not remove it. She was now bound to her world.

Lydee sat up. The hanging vines around her bed twisted, then curled up onto the grassy, green canopy above her. Tiny lights danced on the rough, barklike walls of the cave. Her mentor was not in their room;

she wondered where he had gone.

Reiho is visiting his former mentor, Homesmind's voice said inside her. The voice was soft and gentle, yet insistent; Homesmind sounded as It had when It had spoken to her through a circlet.

Of course I sound the same, Homesmind went on. *The circlet has trained you, and your link will work in the same way. You are now fully a part of this world, Lydee.*

She swung her legs over the side of the bed and stood up. Was Homesmind mocking her? She had lived on Home all her life—Home, the Wanderer, the Forest, the Refuge. People called this world all of those names and it was all of those things, but it was not really her world.

Don't be nonsensical, Homesmind replied to her unspoken thoughts. *Of course this is your world.*

"I don't feel as though it is," Lydee replied. She could not explain her feelings to the world's Mindcore, though she did not have to in any case. Homesmind was undoubtedly sorting through her surface thoughts at that moment. She shut down that particular channel of her link, wanting to keep her feelings, at least, to herself.

Clearing her mind, she phrased her questions: Who am I? Who were my donors? Where am I from? Homesmind showed her only a mist; even now, linked as she was, she received no answers. Her friends had asked the same questions and had seen images of their donors, along with charts of their genetic backgrounds. Each of them carried the genes of several donors; each was the product of centuries of genetic manipulation and modification. They knew who they were. Lydee seemed to have been born from nothing, with no connection to anyone else.

"Where did I come from?" she said aloud. "You've never told me."

Does it matter? You have grown up like all the others.

"It matters to me. Reiho knows, and I'm sure a few of his friends know, and they've never told me, either. Somehow that doesn't seem fair."

You will learn soon enough.

"Tell me now," she insisted.

It is Reiho's task to speak to you, and he is already preparing to do so. It is my hope that you will come to take some joy in the knowledge. Homesmind paused. *Occasionally it is time to bring something new into the world. You may someday have a special task to perform, Lydee.*

She sighed, closing her link. Homesmind could still speak to her when It wished, but would not receive her thoughts.

Her headache had vanished. She crossed the room, took a piece of fruit from a recess in the cave wall, and sat down on one of the giant mushrooms growing from the mossy floor. Homesmind's tone had disturbed her.

Her mentor, she felt, should not have to answer questions Homesmind could have answered.

Where had she come from? She had supposed that her original home was much like this world, that it too was yet another comet transformed ages ago into a garden world, a world in which human beings dwelled inside the giant roots of enormous trees that sprouted from the comet as if the comet were a seed. But she had never seen another comet world, and had not heard of one entering this part of the galaxy in the recent past. Humankind's other comet worlds had voyaged far, and even Homesmind rarely spoke to them. She had learned enough about interstellar distances to understand that her chance of seeing another world like the Forest very soon was remote.

Homesmind had spoken of a special task, but Lydee could not imagine what It would ask of someone like her. Even the oldest adults, those who had lived for centuries and could recall the times when their world had wandered far from this planetary system, had no special tasks and were free to do as they liked. Homesmind cared for them all; It was the brain of her world. Long ago, when human beings had fled to the Halo of comets at the edge of the solar system, Homesmind had been only a small Mindcore, a cybernetic and organic intelligence of colloids and crystals, but during the thousands of years since, It had grown in complexity until no human mind could fully encompass

It. Homesmind had been humanity's child. Now It was their parent, their guardian, their protector, their teacher, their willing servant, and their gentle master. Homesmind was the comet.

Lydee.

She opened her link again. "What is it?"

Nara and Pilo are approaching. Do you wish to visit with them? They are on the path outside.

"I'll meet them there."

Nara's short, white curls fluttered in the breeze. She was wearing a band of gold cloth around her hips, another gold band around her breasts, and the belt everyone wore. Pilo was in a red loincloth. They did not have to walk; the pathway's glassy surface flowed, carrying Lydee toward the girl and the boy as it drew them closer to her. Lydee's cave was one of many on the side of the cliff; the pathway was a narrow foothold.

Pilo grinned. Lydee's breasts shifted, pressing against her band of blue cloth as she waved. She had looked like the others as a child; now her hips were wide and her breasts large. No woman or girl she knew had such a shape; their hips were narrow, their breasts small. She pushed her shoulders forward, trying to flatten her chest.

"Congratulations on your link," Nara sang out as she stepped to the side of the pathway; she was now at the edge. Pilo and Lydee stood near her. Lydee's cave was near the top of the vine-covered bluff; far below, a blue ribbon wound through a green valley. On the other side of the valley, another cliff faced them, striped by the shimmering streaks of the pathways; vines drew away from the mouths of caves as other people left their rooms.

Nara waved at one dark-haired man; Lydee recognized Nara's mentor, Chilon. He signaled to Lydee with his hands. "Congratulations," his voice whispered inside her through her link. She thanked him.

Pilo shook back his thick, black hair, thumbed his belt, floated out from the cliff, then dropped toward the valley below. Lydee and Nara stepped out after him. The white-haired girl fell quickly, arms over her head, her feet pointed; Pilo was diving headfirst. Lydee sat on a pillow of air, then hooked a finger around her belt, slowing herself. A strand of dark hair lashed her eyes; she brushed it away. Nara swooped toward the river, alighted, and sat down on the bank, swirling her pale feet in the water; Pilo landed next to her.

Lydee hovered over the water, then flew toward her friends, scooping up water with her hands. Pilo laughed as she splashed him; droplets glistened on his dark-brown skin. She floated down to him and seated herself.

A tall woman was walking toward the young people, stepping lightly on her toes as if performing a dance. "Genlai," Nara called out, greeting the woman.

Genlai waved at them languidly. Her brown hair was loose around her shoulders; her blue eyes stared past them. "Lydee, you have your link," she said, smiling wistfully. "You'll draw closer to the world as I prepare to leave it."

"Stay," Lydee replied.

"Oh, no." Genlai shook her head. "I'm much too weary. I can welcome death now. I'll say my farewells to you, and go my way." The woman walked on, holding out her arms as if seeking an embrace.

Nara giggled when Genlai was out of sight. "She's preparing to die again," she said, covering her mouth.

Pilo shrugged. "Maybe she means it this time."

"Chilon says she's made her farewells dozens of times, always telling everyone how weary she is, but she always decides to live in the end. I suppose it's her way. She can gaze at the world as if she's seeing it for the last time, and that probably makes it seem more beautiful. It's her little art."

Five small children were on the other side of the river; a tall, slender man was speaking to them. The children sat down and he handed each a thin, silver circlet. As the children put the circlets on their heads, the man pointed toward the colored stones along the bank. One child began to read them.

Lydee could read the stones without Homesmind's help; the position of each bit of rock told the story, which was a simple one about the river's travels through the valley. She gazed at the children; their naked bodies seemed vulnerable, their skin too fleshy, their bones too fragile. As they grew, their skin would gradually be replaced by a stronger, more durable membrane, tiny electrodes would strengthen their muscles, a nearly invisible web of slender wires would encase their skulls, their bones would become like steel. Lydee remembered her own childhood as a time of bruises, aches, cuts, and twinges that had faded as her body acquired the supplements that had made it nearly invulnerable. She stretched out one light-brown hand, flexing her fingers.

A small globe floated toward them, its tray bearing three glasses, a bottle of wine, and a bowl of tidbits. Nara waved at the globe; she had apparently summoned it. The globe settled next to them as Nara poured out the amber liquid; Pilo nibbled at a vegetable cracker.

"To Lydee," Nara sang. "May your new link bind you even more strongly to the world, and to us, and to all who dwell on the Wanderer."

Lydee sipped; Nara had varied the traditional toast a little. " 'Even more strongly.' Are you saying that I need to be bound more than others?"

She had spoken a bit too harshly. Nara's pale-blue eyes widened. "Why, Lydee," she answered softly, "doesn't the link bind everyone more strongly?"

"Of course." Lydee, as usual, had been too clumsy. Eventually she might provoke someone to the raising of a voice, or even an argument, and that would never do. "But you know perfectly well that I was given life elsewhere."

"That doesn't matter."

"Of course it doesn't," Pilo said as he stroked Lydee's hand.

"Some of the oldest people here lived on other comets once," Nara said. "You're no different from them."

"Except that they know where they're from, and I don't."

"You grew up here, and you're here now." That seemed to settle the matter for Nara.

They finished their glasses of wine in silence. Nara seemed preoccupied by the children and their teacher; Pilo was staring calmly at the river. Lydee stretched out, gazing up at the yellow glow above the valley, and was soon lost in a reverie. Her mind soared toward the light. The valley and its cliffs were only a small part of one root, one of the many roots of the giant trees that grew from the comet, spreading their massive leaves in black space to catch the distant light of the sun.

As she closed her eyes, Homesmind showed her the comet as it would appear from a distance, a seed green with life, its bright tail pointing away from the pinprick of light that had made life possible. Other stars dotted the darkness. One small body was not a star, but a tiny blue globe with an even smaller companion. Eons ago, all of humankind had dwelled on that blue, cloudy world, but that world, called Earth, had been abandoned.

The image faded; her peaceful mood had been broken. Reiho and his mentor Etey had seen Earth, had walked on it when Reiho was a boy. They had persuaded Homesmind to remain in the solar system for a time, and they had even spoken to some of Earth's primitive inhabitants.

The presence of humanlike creatures on that world had come as a shock to the cometdwellers, who had believed that no one was left. It was said that the Earth-folk were hardly human at all, that they were barbaric creatures who wanted no contact with the comet. Yet Homesmind remained near that world; Lydee supposed that It wanted to add new facts to Its store of knowledge before traveling on.

She had once asked her mentor about his adventures on humankind's ancient home; the pain in Reiho's eyes had been so intense that she had dropped the subject. Later, he had told her that Earth was best left alone, but she had always known that. It was the world that had driven Home's creators away.

"What are you going to do?" Nara asked. Lydee opened her eyes and sat up; the other girl was pouring more wine. "I only ask because you haven't told anyone, and I was wondering if you'd made up your mind." Nara, as Lydee had expected, was thinking of being a botanist. She had already sketched out some ideas for new floral species, though her mentor Chilon had chided her, in Lydee's presence, for being a bit too garish with her designs. Pilo wanted to do work in brain physiology; his goal was to design an implant that would, as he put it, produce a "perfect and pure transcendence."

"I don't know," Lydee replied, suddenly struck by the fact that all her friends had decided on a life's work, or at least a pursuit that would keep them occupied during their first century, and that she had not been surprised by any of the choices. She remained uncertain. Nara's flowers and Pilo's mental states seemed trivial somehow. She thought of her other close friends; Jerod and his jewelry designs, Tila and her striped butterflies. Lydee wanted to do something more adventurous, but was afraid to admit it, knowing that it would only accentuate her individuality. Everyone prized individuality as long as one was not too distinctive.

They finished the bottle of wine. Nara waved the small globe away, then stood up. "I must get you your gift," she said to Lydee. Thumbing her belt, the white-haired girl drifted up toward the trees bordering the riverbank. Nara's errand, Lydee knew, was only an excuse; her friend had no doubt sensed that she and Pilo wanted to be alone for a while.

The children across the river had been led away. Pilo reached for her hand and held it gently. She smiled. He leaned toward her; her grip tightened as she gazed into his black eyes. He drew back a little.

She was being too intense; her hand had clutched at his too tightly. Blushing, she released him. She had surprised Pilo the first time they had made love. He had expected playfulness, not passion. Even Reiho had warned her against being too emotional. She would have to request more aid from Homesmind in controlling her balance; she slipped into intensity too often.

The boy reached toward her again, taking both hands this time. "It's all right, Lydee. It's what I like about you—you're unpredictable."

"You mean that I'm not like the rest of you."

"Reiho isn't either."

"No, he's not." Her mentor had always been kind and sympathetic, willing to talk to her at any time. She had lived with him for well over three years, ever since she had turned twelve and it had been time to leave the nursery to live with an adult. He had become her lover recently, another responsibility of a mentor when a young charge was more mature, and had counseled her when she spoke of her feelings for others. But there was a part of Reiho she did not know. That was not odd; no one would reveal all of his thoughts and feelings to someone he had known for so short a time. But she had seen the distant look in his eyes before he masked it with a smile. Reiho lived on the Wanderer as if he too were an outsider, apart from others, lost in his own thoughts.

"I've always thought Reiho was awfully young to be

a mentor," Pilo said. "Barely three decades of life. Most are much older."

"I chose him," she answered, wondering if she had. Homesmind had given her several choices, but it now seemed that It had made Reiho seem the most appealing. Perhaps It had thought she would be happier with another who was unusual. "Anyway, he was the first of us to visit Earth since the Flight. That must have counted for something. And you know perfectly well how few choose to be mentors."

Pilo frowned. "That's true. Home has been in balance for a long time. In a way, it doesn't really need us." That unhappy thought was so unlike the boy that she drew back, startled.

"Nara asked what I wanted to do," she said quickly, wanting to change the subject. "But I really don't know." She rested her head against his shoulder. "Maybe I'm supposed to be undecided. Sometimes I wonder if Homesmind wants to send me back to wherever I came from."

"Why would It do that?"

"Think about it, Pilo. How often have we been able to communicate with other worlds?"

"Old ones have done so, and even some younger ones have, not long ago."

"They have contacted some of those who live on other comets and have spoken to them occasionally while viewing images of their worlds. But there's been no physical contact for centuries, even when the comets drew close and visitors could reach another comet easily. We are all human, yet many of those people are as strange as aliens would be."

"You might have been sent here aboard a small vessel. Or the atoms of your body might have been transformed into tachyons and beamed to us while you were still a baby. Homesmind and Its counterparts elsewhere would be capable of that." Lydee nodded; she had considered those possibilities many times. Her link remained silent. Homesmind had long been aware of her speculations, yet It had never confirmed or denied them. "But why would It do such a thing?"

"Because then we could truly communicate with another world and have it understand our ways. I would be able to explain Home to them. Perhaps another world has raised a child from here who will do the same."

"It's possible," Pilo said. "But Homesmind has Its own way of speaking to other worlds, and I wonder—" He bit his lip. "I hope you don't mind speaking of this matter to me."

"If I had, I wouldn't have mentioned it at all." Pilo knew her as well as anyone, yet he was still cautious. Custom dictated distance; too much intimacy was frowned upon, considered trespassing in another's mind. Through their links, it was possible to encompass someone's mind, but such an act was reserved for those who had grown especially close to one another. Lydee, considering all this, could understand why Homesmind might have sought a different way to communicate with another world.

"Reiho knows where I'm from," she went on. "A few others do—his old mentor does. Maybe they don't know enough about that world to tell me much. I must seem impatient to them—most of them have lived for so long. Perhaps people speak freely on that other world, and share their thoughts easily, and don't conceal themselves from one another." She should not have said that; Pilo might be offended.

"Well, Homesmind won't send you anywhere if you don't want to go." The boy reached toward a small pouch at his belt, untied it, and handed it to her. "It's my gift," he said, "to celebrate your link. I want you to have it before the others arrive."

She opened the pouch and took out a small, transparent orb. It twinkled; inside the orb, tiny comet specks circled a sparkling sun. As she held it, her mind seemed to drift after the comets, following them on their journey, another traveler in their company. She put the present back into its pouch, breaking the spell. "It's lovely."

"When you hold it for a long time, you'll feel as though you've become a comet. You'll feel the way Homesmind must feel."

"Lydee!"

The cry came from the river. A boat was rowing itself toward them, its silver oars dipping into the water in unison. Lydee stood up, waving when she saw her friends on its decks. Nara was with them, her hands around the stem of a large, yellow flower. Lydee dived into the water, swimming to the boat.

The yellow flower, Nara's gift, was Lydee's parasol; its stem rested against her shoulder. Tila's present, a silver butterfly striped with red, nestled against one petal. On her wrist, Jerod's bracelet gleamed; the tiny stones on the gold band spelled out a message: You are linked to us. Each stone represented a friend; Tila was amber, Pilo onyx, Nara turquoise, Jerod a diamond. Lydee's stone was black, like Pilo's, but hers was veined with scarlet.

The boat's oars hovered over the water as they drifted. Tila smiled at Pilo's orb of comets, then handed it and the pouch back to Lydee. "Now we all have links," she said, letting her long, brown hair fall over one rosy cheek as she tilted her head.

Jerod handed Lydee a glass of pink wine; the fine silver threads on his bald head glittered in the light. Lydee had known the four on the boat all her life. They had grown up together in the nursery, played together, been taught together, looked after the few younger children together. They would always have a special bond.

"Row on," Jerod said. The boat obediently stroked

the water. They passed a flock of gray waterfowl; the birds lifted their heads in unison. "We should live in boats, not in caves. I dream of a world with rivers and lakes, where we'd never reach shore. We could build a world like that."

"Are you still thinking of doing so?" Nara asked.

"There are too many older ones here," the bald boy replied. "No matter what happens, we'll always be the young ones to them, even after we've lived for a century or two."

Tila shook her head. "By then, some of them will have chosen to give up life."

"Do you really think so? How many old ones ever give up life? How many have given up life since we were incubated?"

Three, Homesmind said inside all of them.

"Three," Jerod continued. "Out of three million."

"It doesn't surprise me," Nara said. "I don't understand why anyone would give up life. Of course, there's Genlai." She giggled.

Jerod's blue eyes narrowed. "She won't choose death. She'll settle for forgetfulness, and then the world will seem new to her again." He draped one lean, muscular arm over his knee. "They won't give up life. And few of them become guides or teachers or mentors, so Homesmind gives us fewer children. You see what I'm saying. It's almost time—time for some of us to leave this world and make a home on another."

Tila gazed at him silently, her hazel eyes lost in

thought. "We can't," she said at last. "We don't know enough."

"We'll know enough before long. Homesmind will help, and give us a new Mind for our new world. Don't you see? That world will be ours. Here, we'll live as those here have always lived. There, we might become something else." His voice was calm, but his eyes shone.

"It could be dangerous at first," Nara murmured. "We'll have to seed another comet."

Jerod shrugged. He had always been more adventurous than the others, the first to attempt new stunts while flying, the first to learn how to pilot one of Home's shuttles. "Not really," he replied in his husky voice. "After all, most of what we'd do would be design. We could wait before moving. I'm sure that some of the younger children would decide to go with us by then."

The prospect appealed to Lydee. *Perhaps it is time,* Homesmind whispered. *This world has not given birth to a new one for centuries.*

"Why talk of it now?" Pilo asked. "We're here for Lydee, to celebrate her link." He reached for a glass.

"That's why I say it." Jerod turned toward Lydee. "Lydee is not like the rest of us." She did not take offense at the statement; the wine had soothed her, and the boy had pitched his voice to convey affection. "You are something new, from another world. You belong to a new world, not to this one."

Lydee considered his words. This was one possibility

she hadn't considered, that Homesmind had been seeking divergence when It had accepted her. It would draw on her genetic pattern to create more children; there would in time be others like her. But there might not be room for them on the Wanderer.

"We should consider your idea," she said to Jerod.

Nara gazed toward shore. "It would be hard to leave Homesmind."

"We'll have another Mind," Jerod responded.

"It will take time," Tila said. "We'll have to go back to the Halo, find a comet, seed it." She laughed. "By then, we'll certainly be old enough to settle there."

"We must consider it," Lydee said, leaning against Pilo. They drifted past a meadow where a large, tawny cat was nuzzling a tiny monkey. Nara began to sing, her crystalline voice accompanied by the lapping of water against the boat.

Reiho was sitting on the floor, his back against a mushroom, the flat rectangle of a reader propped against his knees as Lydee entered their cave. He was frowning, his eyes staring past the reader as if he did not see what was there. Putting it aside, he looked up as she twirled before him, showing him her gifts. The butterfly fluttered to the reader and settled on one of its corners.

"Reiho?" She went to the stocky man and sat down next to him, letting her flower slip to the floor. "What's wrong?"

He shook his head. "Nothing is wrong." His dark,

almond-shaped eyes regarded her solemnly. "Did you enjoy yourself?"

"Of course. We were on the river. We went all of the way to the lake before turning back."

"I have a present for you." Reiho got up, straightened his blue loincloth, and strode to the wall. He took something from one of the recesses, came back to her, and sat down again, folding his legs. There was a blue marble in his open palm.

She took it from him. The marble was a tiny world, blue and green; wispy clouds swept over it as it turned slowly in her hand.

"I must speak to you, Lydee." His voice seemed strained; a line had formed between his black brows. "I've spoken to my old mentor Etey, and Homesmind agrees. It is time you found out who you are."

"Where I'm from." Her hand closed over the marble. "I know who I am." She tried to smile; at last she would know.

"Where you're from and who you are." He ran a hand through his black hair. "It's my duty as your mentor to tell you, hard as it is. You're not from another comet, Lydee."

"But I must be."

"You're from Earth. You're from the world that gift represents. You were born on the world where I died."

2

"No," Lydee said, unable to feel anything except shock. "Only primitives live there, not people like us. Everyone knows that." She let go of the marble; it rolled over the green, mossy floor and came to rest against a mushroom stem.

"They are human, in their way. They're the descendants of those who were left behind when we fled to the Halo."

"Homesmind?" she cried out, suddenly afraid.

Let Reiho speak. I shall aid him if it is necessary. She clasped her hands together.

"You know why our ancestors fled that world," Reiho said.

She nodded. Thousands of years ago, Earth's inhabitants had tried to discover a way to draw on human-kind's latent mental powers. Knowing that some could intermittently read the thoughts of others or move objects with their minds, people had sought a means to amplify those abilities. The human body, by itself, could not contain enough energy to direct those powers; a source of energy had to be found. At last one was.

Reiho and the room faded from view. Lydee was gazing at a grassy plain. The shiny spires of a city gleamed on the horizon as Homesmind showed her Its depiction of Earth's past.

In front of her, the images of men and women watched as golden and crystal pillars rose from the ground. The pillars would be their city of the mind; through the pillars, and the cybernetic minds within them, human beings would have the power to touch one another's thoughts, to move mountains with a wish, to create images out of dust and air. The pillars would channel power to humankind. A new civilization would arise; the human mind would rule all.

The image changed, and Lydee sensed fear. People reeled through the streets of the city as if intoxicated. A man's mind lashed out at a boy, striking him to the ground. A group of women joined their minds, walling themselves off from the chaos around them. A few seized the minds of others, forcing them to dance. Other people were fleeing from the city, pursued by the specters of giants. Still others ran toward the ships that would carry them away from Earth.

Their power corrupted them, Homesmind murmured. *They could not control it. At first, it was a game, and then it became a battle. Hate could no longer be hidden; thought and action were the same.* Several people hurtled through the air, thrown by the minds of their tormentors; others screamed as a building toppled toward them. Lydee felt their despair; they were among those who lacked the mental strength to draw on the power of the pillars, whose minds were deaf and blind to the thoughts of their fellows.

They could not remain on a world where they would be victims, Homesmind said. *The survivors fled to the Halo, where they created new homes among the comets and vowed never to return to Earth.* It did not have to tell her more. The cometdwellers were the descendants of those who had lacked mental powers and who had come to believe that probing too deeply into another's mind could bring only evil.

"No more," Lydee said. She caught a glimpse of pillars being buried under rock as the images of destruction faded. "I know all that. I don't want to see it."

It is important that you do. It is part of your history.

"Some Earthfolk survived," Reiho said. She raised her eyes to his face. "They found a way to live with their abilities. They are taught from childhood how to control themselves, and live out their lives in small villages using only a little of the power available to them. They speak in thoughts instead of words. They believe that their purpose is to draw closer to one another as they grow older until, when they are very old, they can no longer tell which thoughts are their own and which are those of others."

Lydee swallowed. "Then the pillars are still there."

"Oh, yes," Reiho replied. "But they lie buried under mountains and the Earthfolk have forgotten that their ancestors built them. Now they believe that their powers were given to them by a deity. Their brief lives last less than a century, yet they have lived as they do for thousands of years. There are many communities on each of Earth's continents, but they have all followed the same customs."

"All of them? Surely some must have diverged from others in all that time."

He shook his head. "Some live in regions of snow and ice, others are fisherfolk by the sea, and still others tend herds or farms, but their basic beliefs are the same in spite of the distances that separate their communities. Occasionally a few people leave one village for another. They say that this is so they won't grow apart, though it also keeps them from becoming too inbred." He paused. "Curiosity and change are evils to them. They tell legends of the destruction and seek to keep such a thing from happening again. Therefore, their lives are lived out in ignorance. Their customs protect them. Those who are too passionate, who cannot learn control, die out early. All of their young people go through a ritual that eliminates the unfit." He narrowed his eyes. "They think of their world as a peaceful one."

Lydee clutched her knees, drawing them toward her chest. "You said that you died, but you are here, alive. What did you mean?"

Reiho covered his eyes, making her wish she had not asked. "It's hard to speak of it." His voice was low. "The people of one village killed me. They directed their thoughts at my mind, and I had no way to protect myself from that. Etey was with me, but she lived. She stored my lifeless body aboard our shuttle and brought me back here, where Homesmind was able to restore my mental pattern to my body—my memories, my personality, and my thoughts. I live as that Reiho would have lived, but he is gone, and I remember him without feeling that I am he, for I am not." He folded his hands. "I have feared death ever since. The fear seems to grow worse with time. The thread of my life was broken then, and I live here almost as a stranger even now." Loneliness and fear were in his eyes.

Lydee was still, unable to speak for a moment. Her mentor had never revealed so much of himself to her. Homesmind had given Reiho back to his world, but not to himself. Another Reiho lived in the place of that boy, a brother with the same memories. There was something heartless in the way Homesmind had restored Reiho to the Wanderer and to all who knew him, but not to himself.

"You said the Earthpeople were peaceful." She struggled to keep her voice steady. "Why would they strike out at you?"

"They have peace among themselves. But I was an outsider, not part of their world. They feared me. Only one tried to protect me." He reached for her hand. "She was the one who gave you to us."

Lydee was suddenly afraid of knowing more. The image of a girl was before her, a girl with her own curly, dark hair, brown skin, and large bones. The girl wore a dirty white tunic and pants and clutched a baby to her chest. "No," Lydee said, and Homesmind blanked out the image. "Why?" she asked, knowing that she would have to find out.

Reiho squeezed her fingers gently. "Perhaps you should have been told earlier, but Homesmind did not wish it—It thought that such knowledge would only make your childhood more difficult. You see, sometimes even now a child is born on Earth who lacks mindpowers. The people of Earth call such infants 'solitaries' and—" He drew his hand away. "They believe such children are defective. They put such babies to death."

Lydee recoiled. "But that's cruel."

"They feel it is for the best, since such children can't live as they do. They fear those who are separate, as they call it. They also know that such children would be tormented. The temptation to torment the helpless is great." His face was hard. "You were born without mindpowers, Lydee. The Earthgirl who was my friend brought you to Etey because she did not want you to die and knew that you could have a life with us."

"I don't understand," she said, struggling with this new knowledge. "If they don't want such children, why do they have them? Can't they manipulate their genes? Why would they allow a womb to bring forth such a child only to kill it?" Her hands were trembling; she twisted her fingers together.

"They are primitive people. Their powers give them some control over their bodies, but they have never developed the tools we have—they feel no need of them. You were born in the ancient manner. On Earth, a man and a woman make love, their genes combine at random, and a baby is born from the woman's womb."

Lydee stared at him in horror. That she had been born on Earth was shocking enough; she could not endure this final indignity. She was little more than an animal. She had been rejected, given to Home and its people because even Earth's primitives did not want her.

"The girl who gave you to us was your sister," Reiho continued. Her ears were pounding; she could hardly hear him. "That is a word meaning that the man and woman who gave birth to you gave birth to her. She begged Etey to take you."

"You lied to me. Homesmind lied to me all along."

I didn't lie. You always knew you had come from elsewhere. Is it so important?

"I never imagined this." She shrank back from Reiho. "And you became my mentor. Homesmind must have wanted that, too."

Reiho stretched out a hand. "I wanted it. You are like the girl who tried to save me on Earth. I thought you would help me heal."

"How many know what I am?"

"Only a few—you know that. You weren't deceived about that. There's no reason for others to know at this time."

"At this time." She made a fist. "But they'll all know later on."

"Please try to understand," he pleaded. "Homesmind has communicated with Earth's cybernetic Minds. It's learned many things, and It may discover others that could change things for us here. You're a link with Earth—you might help us eventually."

Her head was throbbing; the confrontation was making her ill. She had raised her voice; she was longing to strike out at someone. All her training now seemed only a veneer masking her primitive nature. Her body struggled to restore her balance, dulling the shock.

"You shouldn't have brought me here," she said.

"Your mentor should have refused to take me."

What was Etey to do? Homesmind asked. *Leave you to die? She showed you mercy. A girl on Earth overcame everything she had been taught, and gave you a chance to live. I thought you would be able to understand by now.*

"Don't speak to me," Lydee shouted. "I wish I could tear your link out of my skull."

"Lydee!" Reiho cried.

She jumped up and ran from the cave.

She flew recklessly, far from the valley, frightening other flyers and scattering a flock of birds. By the time she reached the lake, several of those who lived in boats along the shore had gathered on their decks, looking up as she soared overhead. Tiny sailboats skimmed over the water below; she flew on until she spied a small bay. Dropping down, she alighted on the sandy beach. Reiho could, she knew, find her easily enough, but he probably feared another confrontation. Even Homesmind's link had remained silent.

She sat on the sand, gazing out at the graceful sails. A guide had taught her and her friends how to sail when they were younger. She wondered if her friends would have celebrated her link with her if they had known what she was. She had been torn out of a woman's body on a world civilized people had abandoned; that meant she was hardly human at all. She pressed her lips together. Pilo and Nara and the others were too polite to scorn her outright. They would simply withdraw, masking their disdain with cold courtesy. She could not expect them to welcome her on their new world when they found out. Pilo and Jerod would no longer recite love poems to her; Nara and Tila would not invite her to their caves.

She looked down at her round breasts and wide hips, understanding their purpose all too well. Had she remained on Earth, a child might even now be sucking at one breast; an embryo might be growing inside her. A sour taste filled her mouth; she spat into the sand.

A boat was gliding toward her. Two women, tall and bony, adjusted the sail; one waved at Lydee. Their golden skin gleamed.

She stood up, then ran toward them, splashing through the water until it was nearly up to her waist. "Go away!" she screamed. "Don't come near me! I don't want you here!"

One of the pair, apparently frightened, moved too quickly. The sail swung, knocking her into the water. Lydee laughed. The other woman glanced fearfully at the girl, then pressed a finger to her belt and swooped toward her companion. Scooping her up, she flew away quickly. The boat rocked in the water; a breeze caught it, carrying it away from the bay. Lydee's laughter caught in her throat.

She stumbled out of the water and threw herself onto the sand, clawing at it, wishing she could cry.

3

Lydee crawled out from the shade of her tent into the light. A globe bearing food on its tray floated out from under the trees bordering the sandy beach. Another metallic servant, this one a large, golden crab, sat beside the tent. It had brought the tent to her, and she had forgotten to order it away.

Reaching toward the globe as it hovered near her, she accepted a cup of tea, drank it quickly, then waved the rest of the globe's offerings away. She had not eaten for some time. Her body would compensate for that awhile longer, and then she supposed that the crab or one of Homesmind's other servants would force some nourishment on her.

As the globe floated back toward the trees, she thought

she saw someone hiding near one of the pale, white trunks. Limbs covered with feathery green leaves swayed in the breeze. Lydee turned away, suspecting that a few small children or other curious folk were lurking there. Most of the people of Home, she was sure, had never seen anyone so unbalanced. She had screamed at the first group of visitors, chasing them away from the beach, but this had only attracted others to view the spectacle. Rising, she walked down to the water's edge and sat in the wet sand. Here I am, she thought bitterly. Come and look; see the primitive.

She had slept three times in the tent, and did not know how long she had been on the beach. Homesmind had said nothing; even Reiho had not come to see her. They no longer cared what happened to her. Homesmind could wipe the knowledge of her origins from her mind, but eventually she would have to go through the shock of learning about Earth once again.

"Lydee?"

She turned. Pilo was standing by the trees. She raised a hand to her mouth, surprised.

"Lydee?" he said again. "If you don't want me here, I'll go."

She motioned to him. He walked down the beach toward her and sat down several paces away. His black eyes watched her warily; he clutched his elbows as he covered his chest with his arms. It must have taken all of his courage to approach her; she suddenly felt ashamed.

"What do you want, Pilo?"

"Only to speak to you."

"You could have done that through the link. You could have sent your image."

"I thought it might mean more to you if I came myself."

She looked down, poking at the white sand with her fingers. "That was kind of you," she said, beginning to resent his concern. "I suppose Homesmind has told you why I'm upset."

"It has said only that you're disturbed and unhappy. It didn't say more. It didn't even ask me to come here. I don't know what to say to you. To see you like this is hard, Lydee. It disturbs my own balance. I don't understand what could have caused such a thing. Perhaps you need another calming implant."

She lifted her head. "That wouldn't help."

"Why are you here?"

"Are you so sure you want to know?"

"Lydee—I'm your friend. You may tell me whatever you wish. If you want my companionship, I'll stay. If you don't, I'll leave. We're all concerned about you."

"You're the only one here."

"The others are afraid. Jerod would have come, but he was worried that he couldn't maintain his own balance in your presence. They will come here if you ask." His body was tense, as if he were prepared to flee.

"Pilo," she said, "I know where I'm from and what

I am. When you know, you may not want to be my friend."

"I am sure it'll make no difference."

"I'm from Earth." She had said it. His eyebrows rose and his mouth dropped open. "You know that there are still a few primitives there, people who will have nothing to do with us. Reiho and his mentor brought me from that world to this one. I am one of those Earthfolk. I'm sure Homesmind will be happy to tell you the whole sorry tale."

Pilo swallowed, then bowed his head; she could not tell what he was thinking. At last he lifted his eyes to hers. "That cannot affect our friendship. All of us are of Earth in a way, aren't we?"

"You don't understand. The Earthpeople live like animals. Their lives are short. They lack our tools and our knowledge. I didn't even come from a womb chamber as you did—I was expelled from a woman's body."

Pilo started.

"I was given to this world," she continued, "because the Earthpeople didn't want me. I was born without the mindpowers all of them have, and Earthfolk kill such children." The boy's eyes were wide with horror. "I was raised as a child of the Wanderer, but I'm not. My genes were a chance combination—I wasn't even shaped and modified before birth. I don't come from a comet world at all. Earth rejected me, and I don't know if I can ever truly be one of you."

Pilo was clearly struggling with himself. He wrung his hands, glanced toward the lake, then covered his eyes. Shaking his head, he let his hands drop.

"You live here now," he said in a toneless voice. "You grew up on Home, so you are one of us. What you were before doesn't matter."

Her gratitude was tainted with suspicion. Pilo would be too disciplined, too much in balance, to mention his repulsion outright, but he could not hide his feelings completely. He crossed his arms over his chest protectively, watching her through narrowed eyes.

"Is that what you really think, Pilo?"

"How could I feel otherwise?"

She got up and took a step toward him. He threw out his hands, then scrambled up, tripped, and fell. Climbing to his feet again, he raced toward the trees.

"Coward!" she screamed after him. "I see what you really think. Why don't you say it?"

He ran on without answering, disappearing among the trees.

A woman in flight was approaching the beach. Lydee watched as the woman landed gracefully on her feet and recognized the dark-brown skin and frizzy red hair of Reiho's former mentor Etey. She had seen the woman's image, but had never met her in the flesh.

"I greet you, Lydee," Etey said as she drew near.

"What do you want?" Lydee shouted.

The woman seemed unperturbed by Lydee's lack of courtesy and seated herself so close to the girl that Lydee could have reached out and touched her. Lydee glared. Etey's brown eyes were calm; she smiled as she wrapped her slender arms around her long, thin legs. "Why, what do you think I want? I wish to see the girl who is the wonder of the Refuge, who frightens little children with her wildness. I'm as curious as anyone."

"You know what I am. It's your fault I'm here."

"Indeed it is. My fault that you're not dead."

"Where's Reiho? He's my mentor. Why didn't he come here?"

"Why should he? It's obvious you prefer to be alone. Speak to him through your link if you've changed your mind." Etey tilted her head, still smiling. "As a matter of fact, I asked him not to come. He would only have commiserated with you, tried to console you, and fed your self-pity. You are feeling sorry for yourself, aren't you? Why, you could easily restore your balance and allow yourself to grow calm, but apparently you wish to explore these emotions. Poor Lydee. How unfortunate you were to be snatched from death and given a life here."

Lydee clenched a fist. "Leave me alone."

Etey raised an eyebrow. "Chase me away. Go on. You can strike me with that fist, can't you?"

Lydee scowled. "Why bother?"

"Why, indeed?" Etey reclined on one elbow. "So

that you can prove to us all that you're the savage you think you are, I suppose."

"One of my closest friends came to see me," Lydee said. "Even he ran away when I told him what I was."

"Ah." Etey's eyes were unfocused for a moment; she was obviously communicating with Homesmind. "Yes, a boy was here earlier. Do you know what he's doing now?"

"Telling the others what he knows, I imagine."

"Not at all. He's in his room, sorry that he caused you pain by his reaction. He's over the shock and unhappy that he could not console you—so Homesmind tells me. He doesn't know how to make amends."

"I don't believe you, Etey."

"Homesmind will verify what I've said—open your link and see for yourself. I think the boy might be happy to get a message from you."

"I know what Pilo thinks."

Etey sighed. "I know what he is likely to think and what others will think if you go on this way. They'll begin to believe that you *are* a savage, a subhuman. You'll prove it to them. I suppose you must want that. It will certainly make you distinctive. I almost envy you. You can live here, and rail against Home, and be completely free to do whatever you like. No one will ask anything of you, and you'll owe others nothing. You'll be our own wild creature. Well, we can hardly blame you, can we? What else can one expect of a girl with such primitive origins?"

"Go away."

"Poor Lydee. I guess that even Homesmind can make a mistake in judgment. It was so sure you could adapt to life here."

"It's easy for you to talk." Lydee pitched her voice low, trying to show that she could speak calmly. "How would you know what I feel?"

"Oh, I guess I don't, not really." Etey traced a line in the sand. "Right now, I'm thinking of Daiya, the girl who gave you to me. She was about your age at the time. She had to stand up to all her people, at great risk to herself, to try to save Reiho—Reiho as he was then. I'm thinking of him, too. He was the first one of us to communicate with Earth in thousands of years, and he wasn't much older than you are now."

Etey sat up, folding her legs. "Reiho brought Daiya here," she went on. "Her curiosity had made her an outcast, and he hoped she could have a home here. But she could not adapt to our ways. She asked to go back to Earth, and I went there with her and Reiho. I thought I could help somehow." She glanced at the lake for a moment. "I was also curious. But I failed Reiho. He died there, and I could do nothing to prevent it. At least I was able to bring him back here, and you were given to me." She frowned. "I'm thinking of Reiho and Daiya—of their courage. And I'm sorry that you seem to lack it. Perhaps I expected too much."

Lydee looked away.

"That Earthgirl was wild, a girl of strong feelings and intense thoughts. She was your sister—that was what she called it. She wore dirty clothes that hid her body, and I suspect that an occasional insect made a home in her long, tangled hair. With her mental powers, she could fly without one of our belts and could touch the thoughts of others. She could have killed us both, and if Reiho had not been able to break down the wall of fear that first separated them, she would have killed us without a qualm. She was ignorant and superstitious. But she was also brave, and in her own way intelligent. I would have been proud to claim her as one of my people. Of course, she might not have felt the same way about you."

Lydee could not speak.

"You can live here, if you like," Etey continued. "Homesmind will see to your needs. Of course, Reiho and your friends will be unhappy for a bit, but they have many ways to prevent unhappiness and will soon get over it. In the end, they'll pity you, as you pity yourself. Think of that. Why, through your link, you might allow their pity to resonate with yours. That would make for a fine wallow, wouldn't it? Poor thing."

"Be quiet!" Lydee stumbled to her feet and strode toward the lake. Her eyes stung. She managed to squeeze out a tear, wiped her face, and stared at her hand, wondering if Earthpeople were able to cry. Perhaps they cried as untrained children did, shaking as they wept.

She turned around. Etey had summoned a globe and was eating heartily, dipping her fingers into a bowl. First the woman had mocked her; now she seemed indifferent. Lydee stomped toward her. Etey poured a glass of wine and handed it to the girl.

Lydee wanted to throw the glass to the sand; instead, she sat down and sipped the pink liquid. Etey nibbled at a green vegetable spear. "That girl," Lydee managed to say. The woman reached into her bowl for another spear. "Daiya. What happened to her?"

"You wish to know?"

"Yes."

"And I had thought you would be too preoccupied with your own misery to care." The woman poured herself more wine. "She lives near the village where she grew up. Her life has been a hard one, for her questioning of her world's customs has made her an outsider, but her people occasionally speak to her, and sometimes younger ones seek her out. She is waiting for her people to accept what she learned from us— that Earth does not have to keep to its old ways, but can change. Homesmind has watched over her. It can speak to the cybernetic Minds of Earth, and through those Minds It can communicate with Daiya. But she has not spoken to It for a few years now, and Homesmind says that even the Minds housed in the pillars have been silent recently." Etey frowned. "We think of Homesmind as a vast intelligence. But It is a young mind compared to those of Earth. Even It cannot fully encompass Them. Those Minds are also waiting for Earth to change, to awaken from what They see as a long dream." Etey's brown eyes gazed past Lydee.

"Have you or Reiho spoken to Daiya?"

"She didn't want us to. She felt that Earth had to be left alone to find its own way. I believe she was right, but I don't think she'll see much change in her lifetime. The Earthfolk have lived without change for thousands of years, and fear it. Daiya has never asked us to return."

"I don't know if Reiho could," Lydee said. "I think he still fears it."

"I know he does. Anyway, he would be helpless without the mindpowers Earthfolk have. And I cannot return because I have such powers."

Lydee leaned forward. "But how can that be?"

"As some on Earth are born without them, some here are born with them. Homesmind must think such qualities are worth preserving, though I don't know why—we lack the means of using such powers here." Etey shook her head. "On Earth, I heard voices inside me over which I had no control and saw impossible things. I could not hide my thoughts. I would be in danger if I returned."

Lydee was silent. She had only to remain on the

Wanderer and live her life; surely that required little courage.

"I once thought—" Etey paused.

"What did you think?"

"That there might be another reason for your being among us, that Homesmind had a purpose for bringing you up, that you might in time be a bridge to Earth, in a way. But now I think we'll forget Earth, as we did before."

Lydee grimaced. "No one will let me forget."

"Don't be foolish." Etey sounded disdainful. "You'll be a curiosity for a while, that's all. Unless, of course, you are determined to make us remember." She stood up and waved the globe away. "Farewell, Lydee." She pressed her belt and drifted up, flying out over the lake.

This is my home, Lydee told herself, clinging to the thought. She was ashamed of her emotional display; she would prove to everyone that she was no different from any civilized being. Earth was only a name. When she was as old as Etey, her origins would no longer seem as important.

"Take down the tent," she said to the golden crab.

At last, Homesmind whispered. *I was afraid you might persist in your self-imposed exile.*

"No," she said. "I'll go home now."

4

She was in a desert. The air shimmered, rippling the
flat, dry land; the sun seemed to fill the sky. Bones
were strewn on the ground; mounds of dirt hid other
bodies. A large bird perched on a skull and stared at
her with beady eyes. Lydee screamed.

She was awake, back in her bed. She forced her eyes
open; if she closed them, she would find herself back
in the desert. Arms held her.

"Lydee," Reiho's voice said in the dark, "what's
wrong?"

She clung to him, her fingers digging into his arm.
"I'm all right." Her body was growing calmer; she
relaxed. "Homesmind will have to provide some dreams
for me—I can't sleep with my own. I keep seeing
Earth."

She stretched out again. The bed's surface flowed under her, cradling her. Reiho held her hand.

"Perhaps you shouldn't have viewed it," he said at last. "You knew what you needed to know. You didn't have to experience those things."

"I had to try. I won't anymore. I know why Earth frightens you now."

Earlier, Homesmind had shown her part of Daiya's life. It had stored the Earthgirl's experiences inside Itself along with the records of the lives of Home's inhabitants It had always kept. But Daiya, unlike the cometdwellers, had not shielded her deepest feelings from Homesmind, and It had recorded them as well.

Lydee had not only seen Earth through Daiya's eyes, but had also touched her emotions. She had viewed only a few incidents before closing her link, but the images persisted: sheer-faced mountains hiding the pillars holding Earth's cybernetic Minds, a village of huts with grassy roofs, people with physical deformities—thinning hair, wrinkled faces, sagging bodies. Worst of all had been the desert, where some of Daiya's friends had died undergoing the rite the Earthfolk called an "ordeal." The emotions of rage, fear, and despair had underscored the visions.

"She cared for you," Lydee murmured. "I saw enough to grasp that. But there was one she longed for, a boy in her village. It felt almost as if she wanted to swallow him, to make his thoughts hers. Love is an illness there." Even her own feelings had never been that strong.

"Perhaps." Reiho sighed. "And yet I sometimes feel I can understand it."

Lydee could not. She had felt what she called love for Pilo and Jerod and Reiho himself, but they would all love others as well. Earthpeople formed pairs, reaching out to others only when they were old; that much she had understood from Daiya's thoughts.

"Once," her mentor continued, "that young Reiho thought that this world and Earth would grow closer, that we would learn from one another. We would give them our science, and they would offer their visions, their dream of being united in one vast mind. He even believed that a way might be found for those of us without powers to acquire them. But he was only a boy."

"It might still happen." Even as she spoke, she heard the insincerity in her voice. Daiya's own mother and father, a woman named Anra and a man called Brun, had been willing to have their own child die to preserve Earth's ways; she had seen that much in Homesmind's re-creation of Daiya's life. If Earthfolk would sacrifice their own young in such a cause, they were hardly likely to reach out to cometdwellers.

"We should have left this system," Reiho said. "There's nothing for us here. It would have been easier for you, too. Earth would be distant."

"I may leave this system anyway. My friends think we should seed our own comet." She paused. "But they might not want me with them now."

"Oh, they will." He stroked her hair. "Sleep, Lydee. Dream other dreams."

The shuttle dropped toward Home. The comet's tail pointed away from the sun; the Wanderer would soon cross Earth's orbital path once more. A jungle of giant trees obscured the distant blue globe.

Lydee glanced at Pilo, who was at her side. He had been gazing intently at Earth before the comet's trees had blocked it from view.

"Do you ever want to go to Earth?" he said casually. "I mean, now that you know." He cleared his throat.

"I certainly don't."

"Not that I think you should, of course." His voice sounded almost too earnest.

"They don't want any of us there in the first place, and it would be dangerous. You've viewed what Homesmind knows about Earth, haven't you?"

"No, I haven't viewed it." She turned toward him, surprised. He smiled. He smiled whenever she looked at him, as Jerod and Nara and Tila smiled. She was beginning to dislike their solicitude. They smiled so often and spoke so gently in their efforts to show her that they still cared for her that she was starting to think she was being patronized. Perhaps they feared her, deep down. "I doubt I'll ever look at those records of Earth," Pilo finished.

"Why not?"

"They really don't interest me." His smile widened.

She turned away. He did not have to explain it; she could guess why he hadn't looked. He could accept her story of her origins and dismiss it, at least consciously; it had been only words. But if he viewed Earth through Daiya's eyes, he would see Lydee only as another savage and would never be at ease with her again. He had already seen how easily she could fall into a primitive state during her time by the lake.

Another shuttle darted in front of them, then fell toward the trees. Jerod was piloting that ship; he often overrode the shuttle's piloting system to take control himself. The small, domed vehicle dipped toward a leaf, becoming a speck against the green; one of its long runners brushed against the leaf. Lydee watched calmly. Jerod was in no real danger; the shuttle's pilot would take over if he grew too reckless.

Her link hummed softly as her own ship passed through an opening in the energy field surrounding the comet; the field closed behind her. Only light could penetrate the field that protected the Wanderer. Her shuttle fell past leaves and stems; mirrored surfaces gleamed among the green. Through the tree limbs, oxygen was channeled into the trunks and then down to the roots in which the people of Home lived. The broad leaves captured sunlight; the roots drew moisture from the comet they entwined. Long ago, the comet-dwellers had kept within the solar system, dependent on the sun's light, but in time innovations had made it possible for the trees to store their energy and for people to control a comet's path. They had been able to travel at speeds faster than light throughout this part of the galaxy for hundreds of years, replenishing their energy as they orbited other stars. Space was their ocean, the stars their ports.

The leaves had vanished; they were now among tree trunks. Through her link, Lydee felt as though the shuttle was part of her, an extension of her body. She took control for a moment, circling a trunk before continuing to fall. The shuttle swooped toward a root, approaching a tiny, lighted space which grew into a lighted cave and then a large, bright room. They flew on, soaring through a wide passageway until they came to a plain of grass, where they landed next to a field of shuttlecraft.

The doors of the shuttle slid open; Lydee and Pilo jumped out. Jerod had already landed; he hurried toward them, taking Lydee's arm. She offered her other arm to Pilo. A dark-haired woman was climbing into one shuttle; she stared at Lydee, who tensed. Those living in the caves near hers had stared at her in the same way, as if they had never seen her before, when she had returned from the lake.

They crossed the shuttle field, moving toward the garden that bordered it. The flowers nodded at them as they drew near; one red blossom detached itself from its stem and floated toward them. Jerod released her, caught the rose, bowed, and presented it; Lydee tucked it behind her ear.

She sat in the grass near one flower bed; Pilo and Jerod sat near her. The two boys were smiling again, showing their teeth. Jerod touched her hand, then glanced at Pilo; the dark-haired boy got up and wandered away.

"I'm better at piloting," Jerod said. "The shuttle rarely overrides me now."

"Good for you." She too was smiling, feeling as though her face would crack.

"We could take a shuttle to Earth's moon. No one would mind that. We could explore the ruins, the catacombs."

"It wouldn't be wise even to go there."

Jerod's smile faded. His blue eyes gazed at her a little too intently, and she looked away. Pilo had disappeared among the flowers.

"They read minds on Earth," Jerod murmured. "They don't just link to have conversations, or exchange surface thoughts—they can touch all of a mind."

"So can people here." She wondered why he had mentioned it. "Some old ones link that way sometimes."

"Earth is different. I've seen what Homesmind knows. I've seen the record of the one who gave you to this world. I never knew a mind could be so wild, could feel so much."

She was suddenly afraid. Before she could reply, Jerod grabbed her, clawing roughly at her arms. She tried to twist away. He pinned her to the ground, gripping her shoulders; his jaw tightened. He was probing her link, trying to touch her thoughts. She closed the link, but not before she had flooded him with her fear. Reaching up, she pushed him away with one shaking hand.

He sprawled on the ground, covering his face. "What are you doing?" she cried out.

"I wanted to—" He shook his head. A man and a woman were strolling toward them; the man glanced at Lydee and Jerod, took the woman's hand, and led her hastily away toward a lattice of vines. "I wanted to touch your thoughts. Forgive me, Lydee. I didn't know what I was doing. The images of Earth must have infected me somehow."

"It wasn't that," she replied. "It was me. I'm just another Earth creature to you—that's how you see me now."

"Oh, no. I'm in balance now. It won't happen again."

She stood up. "No, it won't. I won't let it." She thumbed her belt and rose from the ground.

"Wait," Jerod called out, floating after her. "Don't

be angry with me. Please say you'll forget." He flew at her side, gesturing plaintively with his hands. She reached for the flower he had given her, letting it flutter from her fingers; the blossom drifted toward the ground.

She flew on, Jerod following her. At last he dipped toward the ground and she soared on, alone.

As Lydee entered her cave, she saw that Reiho had a visitor. Her mentor sat on one mushroom, legs folded; Etey was seated on the ground near him.

"I was about to call to you," Reiho said.

Lydee sat down across from him. "I've just found out how my closest friends are going to treat me from now on. I suppose they couldn't hide their feelings forever. Pilo's still afraid of me, though he won't admit it. But Jerod isn't afraid anymore—he'd like his own pet savage." Realizing that she was glaring at the two, she tried to compose herself.

"Forget your petty problems," Etey said. "We have more important matters to concern us now. Your problems will pass."

Lydee turned toward Reiho, noticing the worried look on his face. "What is it?" she asked, suddenly concerned.

"Daiya has called to Homesmind from Earth. She seeks Its aid." Reiho frowned. "She believes her village is now threatened."

Lydee lifted a hand to her mouth. "But how?"

"Recently, her people have tried to touch the minds of other people in other villages. In order to do that, the older villagers, those whose minds are strongest, must link their thoughts and reach out to others far away. They have not been able to do so since Etey and I left Earth, but a short time ago, they managed to contact a village far to the north. As soon as the people there touched the thoughts of Daiya's people, they broke off the contact."

"Why would they do that?" Lydee asked.

"Because they believe Daiya's village to be contaminated. The people there had contact with us, you see, and we are believed to be an evil. 'Separate selves,' they call us, beings who cannot touch other minds and become part of what they call a 'Net.' The other villages of Earth fear being infected by our evil."

Reiho glanced at Etey, who was watching Lydee dispassionately. "Daiya has now discovered that there is a wall around her village, an invisible barrier," Reiho went on. "No one can move more than three or four days' travel from the town. She thinks that the other villages have placed the wall around them, and she fears what may happen next."

"Can't Homesmind help them?" Lydee asked, worried in spite of herself.

"The Minds of the pillars will watch over the village, I am sure," Etey replied. "Homesmind can do little. But Daiya's people are afraid. They know that Daiya has called to us. They must be very frightened to have allowed that, for they are still suspicious of us, and wary."

Lydee's concern was fading; Earth's troubles had nothing to do with her. "But we can't help them."

"She has asked Reiho to return," Etey said. Reiho was staring at the floor; his hands were trembling.

"But what can he do?"

Reiho stood up and began to pace the room. "I can't," he whispered. "My former self died there. The thread of my life was broken there. I fear it too much." He looked up. "She calls for a Reiho who no longer exists."

"You can't go, then," Lydee said. "She must understand that. You can't help her. Let them take care of themselves."

Etey gazed at Reiho. "Lydee is right. You should stay here. Of course, the fear will still be with you. You'll run from it rather than face it. You think you can escape it here." She shrugged. "Someone else died, not you—believing you did is an illusion. Well, you'd be of no use there. Tell Daiya you must stay here. She asked us not to interfere before, so remind her of that and tell her that she must fight her own battles. She still has the Minds of her world to help her."

Reiho glared at his former mentor. "You're saying I'm a coward."

"I know you are. The Reiho who died wasn't. That

in itself proves that you are not he."

"She didn't ask you to return, Etey."

"That's true. So of course my words mean nothing. Isn't that so?"

Lydee crossed her arms, disturbed by the open show of anger. "Reiho's my mentor," she said. "He should stay here, with me. I doubt that anyone else will especially want to replace him, and I'd rather not live alone."

Someone will have to go, Homesmind whispered inside all three of them.

Etey started; Reiho sat down abruptly.

The Mindcores of Earth have not spoken to Me for some time, Homesmind continued. *They have not shared everything with Me and have been silent about recent events. I do not understand this, and would like to have one linked with Me present on Earth.*

"But you can speak to Daiya," Reiho said.

That is true. The Mindcores there have left a channel to Their power open, though Their voices no longer speak to Me, and through that channel, I can hear Daiya. But there is always a chance that that link will be broken. I wish to observe Earth, especially now. One linked to Me should travel there.

"Don't ask this of me," Reiho pleaded.

There is another who could go. Lydee is Daiya's sister. Daiya will accept her in Reiho's place.

Lydee gasped. Reiho seemed stunned. Etey's brown eyes were cold, as always.

"She's hardly more than a child," Reiho said. "You can't ask that of her. Surely out of all the people here, you can find someone else."

The old ones could not endure having their thoughts revealed to the Earthfolk, and the younger ones would be strangers to Daiya. She needs one who might be a friend. If you are so concerned for Lydee, then go to Earth yourself, or accompany her there.

Reiho covered his brow with one hand; Lydee could see his shame. He might argue with Homesmind, but he would not act.

I knew that Earth could not remain as it is, Homesmind went on. *I did not expect anyone to call to Me so soon, but it has happened. Perhaps it is time, Lydee. You once imagined that you might return to the world that was once your home.*

"That was before I knew it was Earth."

Does that matter?

"You knew," Lydee said. "You knew all along that you were going to send me back someday."

I suspected that it might be necessary.

She was only Homesmind's puppet. She and everyone linked to It were no more than Its eyes, ears, limbs, and organs. It only let them believe their lives were their own until It had need of them.

"You can't force me to go, Homesmind."

That is true. I can only ask. But do you feel that you can ever be at peace here until you come to terms with the world where you were born?

"Of course I can," she replied, wanting to believe it.

Stubborn child. Homesmind's words stung. *You might be the link through which Home and Earth could be bound together. Earth was your world. Do you owe nothing to the one who gave you to Me? Can you forget those like you who are still put to death on that planet?*

She covered her ears, though she could not silence Homesmind that way.

You have seen Reiho's fear. You will acquire your own fear, which will grow more intense the more you hide from it. I have prepared you for a journey, though you do not realize it. It paused. *Now I must show you My discovery. Do you see the bottle on the table there before you?*

She looked at the crystal bottle, which stood on a piece of wood resting on thick stems. "Of course."

I have opened a channel in your link. Concentrate on that bottle. Lift it with your mind without grasping it with your hands.

Lydee almost laughed. "But that's impossible."

Try.

Etey fidgeted; Reiho seemed puzzled. Lydee gazed at the bottle. An invisible tendril seemed to flow from her; the bottle suddenly raised itself. She cried out. It hovered over the table, then fell to the ground, rolling toward her.

Etey's eyes were wide. Reiho was staring at the bottle.

Lydee was afraid even to think, fearing what might happen next.

I've closed the channel now, Homesmind said. *Your mind is as it was.*

"How did that happen?" Etey asked; her voice was shrill. "It isn't possible."

Reiho shook his head. "I can guess. Homesmind has somehow channeled power from Earth's Mindcores to Lydee." He paused. "But Lydee has no powers. She shouldn't be able to draw on the power of those Minds."

I have found a way. In every human mind, there is such ability. In some, it is so weak that it cannot function, cannot even be perceived by the Earthpeople themselves. Such people need an implant to aid them, as someone without an arm would need a prosthesis. Theoretically, I could now channel such power to everyone here, though in fact it is beyond My present capacities. Lydee has just demonstrated my discovery.

Reiho was pale. "I had once hoped Homesmind might be capable of this. Our minds and those of the Earthfolk are so similar that I thought a way might be found to give us the powers they have. Now it seems we've had them all along."

"It's deceived us," Etey said. "It told us nothing of Its investigations. We don't need such powers here. They'll destroy us, as Earth was nearly destroyed."

Don't you understand? Homesmind murmured.

Lydee could sense Its distress. *Your ancestors were re-jected and despised by Earthfolk because they believed you lacked the powers common to all of them. But if they learn otherwise, they may come to accept you. And Lydee will not be helpless on Earth. Through this new channel, she will, while on Earth near the Mindcores there, be able to draw on power from Them directly, without My intercession. Do you see?*

"Now I know I can't return to Earth," Reiho murmured. "My fear would touch the minds of everyone there through such a channel." He brushed back a lock of black hair. "And You cannot send Lydee. She would have to confront people who are skilled in the use of those powers, while she is not."

She can be trained. But there is not much time. The Earthfolk are human beings, and so are you. You have diverged from one another long enough. Perhaps it is time you drew together. Ignorance breeds fear. If you believe knowledge is a good, then you cannot reject this knowledge because you find it inconvenient.

Lydee picked up the bottle, turning it in her hands. The room faded. She was lying on her back, squinting at bright light; where had the darkness gone? Two fleshy blobs hovered overhead; a gaping hole appeared in one. Someone was crying. A claw was squeezing her mind; she cried out as the light collapsed into blackness and knew she was dying.

She was back in her cave, stretched out on the mossy

floor. Reiho was kneeling over her. Her right hand clutched pieces of glass; she had crushed the bottle. Reiho brushed the shards from her uncut hand.

That is how infants on Earth still die, Homesmind said. *That is how you would have died if you hadn't been given to Me. Are you content to let it go on happening when you might prevent it?*

She sat up, leaning against Reiho for a moment, then climbed to her feet. "I must consider this," she murmured. Her fear was gone, replaced by a feeling of helplessness and a gnawing anxiety. "I can't decide now."

"Lydee, let me help," Reiho said.

"You can't." You've failed me, she wanted to say. You'll let me go and be glad it's not you who are going. She walked toward the mouth of the cave; the vines let her pass.

She sat by the river, recalling her recent celebration. She had been happy then, and had not fully appreciated it at the time. Let me go back, her thoughts whispered to Homesmind. Erase what I know now— let me wonder about my origins without knowing. One can be happy in ignorance, in spite of what You think.

Homesmind did not reply.

Her link hummed softly. A ghostly shape shimmered near her, becoming the image of Jerod. Other images took shape, becoming Nara, Tila, and Pilo.

"May we speak?" Jerod asked through her link.

She nodded, keeping her mind still so that her friends would hear only her words and not her deeper thoughts.

"Homesmind has said that you might have need of us now."

"Well, It's wrong. You can't help me."

"Lydee, we are your friends."

"Are you?" She did not wait for an answer. "Homesmind has asked me to return to Earth. Let It tell you what It told me."

"It has already done so," Nara said.

"I see. It will use everyone here to force me to go."

"No," Tila responded. "We're not speaking for It, but for ourselves. We'll be your friends, whatever you decide. Homesmind is asking a lot of you, and It may be asking too much."

"Would you go with me?" Lydee asked. "Would you go to Earth knowing that your mind, all of it, would be open to the thoughts of others? Would you travel to a world where people kill and think nothing of it? You might die there yourselves, as Reiho did." She wrapped her arms around her legs, resting her chin on her knees. Nara's face was drawn; Pilo was shading his eyes. "You are thinking I speak too openly. I don't have to look inside you to know that. You've already seen more of my feelings than is customary. But this is nothing compared to what happens on Earth."

"I would go," Jerod said. The others clearly had not

heard him; he was speaking only to Lydee. "You may do something that will live on in the minds of those who will follow us, not just in Homesmind's memories. I doubt that I shall. Don't condemn the others because they can't."

"It's the risk that attracts you, Jerod."

"It's more than that."

Tila whispered a farewell, then vanished; Nara's image disappeared. Pilo lingered, then was gone.

Jerod said, "I would go in your place if I could. But Homesmind says that this is not a task for me. I would do it for you, Lydee."

She sat up, moved by the emotion in his words. "Your feelings are strong."

"No stronger than yours. We have both been well trained to hide them." He frowned. "I have said too much."

"No, you haven't."

"I see now that I have traits I might never have become fully aware of if I hadn't known you, and what you are. I have wondered why Homesmind created me as I am, making me a little more reckless and discontented than others. Now I know. This world might change, and we'll be part of that change. People willing to take risks might be needed."

Her mouth twisted. Perhaps Homesmind had created Jerod for only one purpose—to force her along on the journey It had always known she would have to make someday. The boy was probably speaking for Homesmind now without realizing it.

"I see that I'll have to go," she said. With those words, her anxiety faded; the decision had been made. "You'll probably say I have a great adventure in store."

"But you do."

She smiled at his romantic notions; he would never have to test them against reality. "And you'll think that I'll discover that I'm braver than I thought."

"That might be so."

She rose. "I may only find out that I'm really like everyone else here after all." She laughed joylessly. "That *is* what I've always wanted."

5

Earth swelled as Lydee's shuttle dropped through the clouds. The ground below rushed up toward her; the shuttle suddenly veered to the right, evading a barrier.

A *force field,* Homesmind murmured. A diagram flickered in her mind and on the shuttle's screen. The field, reaching above the stratosphere, was an invisible wall enclosing green land, part of a mountain range, and a small bit of desert. Lydee shivered; the force field showed how much power Earthfolk could summon. She would be trapped inside its borders, along with Daiya and her village.

The shuttle fell toward the desert, landing inside the transparent barrier. She peered through the ship's dome. The shadows of the barren mountains cloaked her craft;

behind her, the desert stretched to the horizon, a barren landscape dotted by only a few prickly plants.

She huddled against her seat. Up until the moment she had left the comet, she had been hoping that Reiho would overcome his fear. He had talked to her of going, and had even tested the mindpowers Homesmind could now give to him.

He had come to the shuttle field with Etey, but had not boarded the craft. "I need more time," he said as he turned away. Etey gripped him by the shoulders and said, "He'll join you," but Lydee had not believed it, and it was too late for her to turn back.

She lifted her hand. Her friends had said farewell at her cave. She gazed at the blue stone in the ring they had given to her. They had accepted her decision; better that she, who had come from Earth, should take the risk of establishing contact with that planet. All the years of believing that she would be fully part of Home had been an illusion. She was expendable.

Homesmind had told her to land in the desert; Daiya had wished to meet her away from the village. Lydee struggled with herself, afraid to step out under open sky. Homesmind had prepared her as well as It could, leading her through images of Earth that had seemed as real as the scene before her, but this was not an image. She would not be able to close her mind to it and find herself back in her cave.

She took a breath, then noticed that two figures,

partly shadowed by the recess in which they stood, were standing on the mountainside in front of her. The shuttle's sensors showed that they were human. She frowned, wondering who they were; she had thought that she would meet Daiya alone.

"Homesmind?" she called out.

They are two from Daiya's village. She is nearby.

Lydee had not yet spoken to Daiya; the woman had relayed her brief instructions through Homesmind. The Earthwoman might also be apprehensive about their meeting; perhaps she was disappointed that Reiho had not come.

The two strangers leaped from their ledge, floating down toward her. They alighted gracefully, then sat down. One was a boy with reddish-brown hair that fell to his shoulders; the other was a girl with auburn curls. At least she assumed that was what they were; their clothing concealed so much of their bodies it was hard to be sure.

The shuttle door slid open. She stepped out, jumping the short distance to the ground.

The disorientation she had felt inside the shuttle was intensified. The air was thick, alive with sounds, whistling as the wind gusted past her. Carefully, she opened the channel to Earth's Mindcores. Her body seemed to swell as the power rushed into her, a stream of strength and will. Homesmind had trained her to use this power, but she had not felt its full force before.

She kept her mind still. I haven't had enough time, part of her murmured to Homesmind. You trained me too hastily. Take me back.

—Go back, then— a voice said inside her.

Lydee tensed. Someone else had heard her thoughts. She narrowed the channel, trying to concentrate. The Earthpeople rose and began to walk toward her.

She raised a hand in greeting, waited until they were a few paces away, then sat down, telling herself she had nothing to fear. Homesmind had shown her how to put a wall around her thoughts, and the silver lifesuit clinging to her body would protect her from physical harm. Such things had not helped Reiho. She repressed that thought.

—Can you mindspeak?— the voice asked.

"I can," she said aloud in the language Homesmind had taught her, the language of Earth. "But it is still hard for me."

"Then we must use words," the boy replied, "and speak to you as we speak to a child who has uncontrolled thoughts." Sensing his disdain, she raised a mental wall to shield herself. The boy's eyes were brown, the girl's a startling green. But there was a resemblance between them; they had the same round face, strong chin, and slender nose. They were clothed in brown tunics and pants; their feet, she noticed, were covered with leather slippers called moccasins. She swallowed; Earthpeople took leather from the hides of dead animals. She tried not to think of that.

"We were told that you are called Lydee," the girl said. "You were born a solitary but were saved from death and sent to live in the sky. You are Lydee AnraBrun."

"Only Lydee."

"Anra LeitoMorgen is your mother and Brun RillaCerwen is your father. That means you are Lydee AnraBrun, doesn't it?"

Lydee shrugged. Homesmind had told her of this custom; now she would have to get used to a name that would only remind her of how sordid her origins were. "Who are you?"

"I am Luret NenlaKal." The girl gestured at the boy. "This is my mother's brother, Marellon BariWil, but we are nearly the same age and grew up together—we even passed through our ordeal together, so we are almost brother and sister ourselves."

"Nenla raised me," the boy said coldly, "after our parents left this life. They couldn't endure thinking that we might have to abandon old ways, and lost the will to live." He glared at Lydee, as if blaming her for it; she shrank at such an open display of emotion.

"Daiya has told us of you," Luret said, "that you live in the sky with other separate selves and were once a separate self also, but no longer are."

"True enough," Lydee said, though she would not have put it that way. "We do not have to be separate now. The ones you call separate selves or solitaries can be given your powers and taught how to use them. In fact, we all have them—it's just that they are very weak in some."

"Daiya's told us that, too," the boy Marellon said. "It means that one of her questions has been answered. Daiya once believed that God was cruel to create separate selves. Now she knows, through the Mind of your world, that God has given powers to all."

Lydee tried not to frown at that reminder of Earth's superstitions. "How much do you know of my world?"

"What Daiya has told us and shown us—that you live on a world of trees in the sky, and that its fiery tail, which we can see when you pass, does not consume it." Marellon waved a hand. "All in our village know of you, but most have tried to forget."

"Then you are much like my people," she said sourly.

"We try to live as we have always, but our knowledge of you festers and makes us doubt. Daiya must live apart from us because she reminds us of this unwelcome knowledge. Few seek her out, and there are those who still curse her. We are two who have learned from her, but I must tell you there are times when we wish we hadn't."

Lydee was uneasy. She had first seen the two only a few moments ago, and already they were speaking of their feelings honestly.

"Our knowledge is a curse," Luret murmured. "Now it divides our village from the rest of Earth, and has even divided us from one another. Perhaps we should have cleansed our minds of it, but then Daiya would always be there to remind us." She got up. "Come with me."

Lydee followed the girl, Marellon at her side. Her nose wrinkled; she could smell the dirt and sweat on their bodies. Homesmind had not prepared her for Earth's odors. She gazed out at the desert, wondering where Luret was leading her.

The Earthgirl stopped abruptly and held out her hands. "Do you feel it?"

Lydee stepped forward, bumping into an invisible shield; they had reached the barrier. She pushed against it with her hands, but could move no farther.

"That's the wall," Luret said. "It stretches out across the desert and over the mountains yonder. It surrounds our village and our lands on all sides, and we're trapped behind it. We can't go through it, and we have tried, summoning all our power. Perhaps if we flew as high as your machine there does, we could escape it—it can't reach to the stars—but we are not able to fly so high."

"Can't you call on the power of your Mindcores?"

Luret shook her head. "Our bodies weaken too quickly when we call on too much power, and we can't sustain the assault. And we're afraid that the wall would only be replaced with a stronger wall. So we wait, to see what will happen."

Marellon kicked at the barrier. "I think the Minds

under the mountains have abandoned us. Their power remains, but They no longer speak, even to Daiya." He glared at Lydee; she sensed his anger and despair. "I don't know why you're here. You can do nothing. Let your sister see you and then go back to your accursed world. You'll only bring more harm to us, and some in the village will not welcome you."

"I was asked to come," Lydee said evenly. "I didn't choose it by myself."

"I see that you are useless. Daiya will see it, too. She should never have called to your world." He turned and strode toward the mountains.

"He shouldn't have said that to you," Luret murmured.

"He's probably right."

The two girls walked back to the shuttle. Marellon was seated near one runner, gnawing at a piece of food. Luret sat down next to him, took a knife from her belt, opened a pouch, and took out a reddish-brown mass, cutting at it with her knife. She held out one dirty hand; a brown bit of food lay in her palm.

"Take it," Luret said. "We can share our food with you. It's dried meat."

Lydee recoiled, remembering that these people were flesh-eaters. She tried to smile; the girl was only being friendly. "I don't want your food. I have a synthesizer and packages of food in my vessel." That sounded too harsh. "Thank you for offering it, though." She tried not to watch them as they ate, afraid she might be sick.

Marellon finished his meal, cleared his throat, spat, and began to rub at his teeth with one finger. Lydee stared past him at the mountains. What did Homesmind expect her to do here? The two young people, with their dirty clothes and crude habits, repelled her, and she was sure that she looked as strange to them in her skintight silver suit.

—Yes, you do— a voice said. —You look more like a machine than a person—

She had forgotten to shield her thoughts and quickly hid them again, leaving only a small pathway. —I am not yet used to this world— she said with her mind.

"You are a poor mindspeaker," Marellon said aloud. "You fondle each word as if you're afraid to let it go." He stood up, wiping his hands on his tunic. "We'll take you to Daiya."

"Is there a place near where we're going for my shuttle to land?"

"Must you cling to that vessel as a child clings to its mother? You may leave it here—or will it fly away without you?" The boy's hostility warmed the already hot air. "We're not going far."

"I had thought those who could touch other minds would know more about courtesy and show more sensitivity to others." Lydee narrowed her eyes. "But I suppose you don't yet see me as a person like yourselves."

"That's true," Marellon replied. "And you're repelled by us. You can't hide it. Your courtesy would only be a lie."

Luret pulled at Marellon's hand while gazing at him reproachfully, then turned toward Lydee. "You must go there," she said, pointing to a rocky ledge above them. "It is wide enough there for your vessel to land. Go, and wait for us."

The shuttle sat on the ledge in front of a cave. Lydee stood beside it and watched as Luret and Marellon ascended the mountain. The two were moving slowly, climbing, then floating up a short distance to a foothold, then resting before going on.

She knew that the Earthfolk, even with their powers, had to conserve their strength; a body could be exhausted by the exercise of the mind. The Earthpeople were frail, their bodies unmodified; she was suddenly aware of the strain in their muscles, the pumping of their hearts, the panting of their lungs. They needed their mental powers to compensate for their physical weakness. She wondered what the boy and the girl were thinking. It would be easy enough to find out, but she did not want to feel Marellon's antagonism again.

She adjusted the pack on her back. Not knowing how long she might be inside the mountain separated from her ship, she had prepared a pack of supplies:

water, food, a few small tools. At her waist, attached to her belt, she carried a small, cylindrical weapon that could stun, but not kill, living things. It would be of little use against people, who might read her intentions before she could use it unless she was very good at shielding her thoughts, but Earth's animals were not so tame and gentle as those on the Wanderer, and she would have to be on guard. She frowned; Daiya might be offended at the weapon's presence. She thought of leaving it behind, then remembered that the two young people were carrying knives; Daiya might have one, too. These people were only too accustomed to death.

Marellon was now just below her. He drifted up, floated over the shuttle's dome, and disappeared; Luret followed him. Lydee thumbed her belt and floated over the craft, landing at the cave's entrance.

Luret led her inside: Marellon had been swallowed by the darkness. They shuffled through a long passage, the Earthgirl guiding her by the elbow; Lydee tried not to think of the dirt she had seen under Luret's nails.

"It isn't far," Luret whispered.

She could no longer hear Marellon. Cautiously, she sent out a tendril of thought and touched him. His hostility had become a thick, soupy resentment laced with scorn for Lydee's need to carry supplies on such a short journey.

—You should have told me I didn't need them— she thought. His wall came up, hiding his thoughts.

Luret pulled at her, signaling her to stop. She heard a hum as metal scraped against rock; the ground shook slightly. The passage was suddenly illuminated by a dull light; the wall in front of them had opened.

They entered a large chamber; the walls around them brightened into gold. A gap separated part of the floor from the opposite wall. Lydee followed her companions to the gap and found herself gazing down a tunnel hundreds of paces deep.

"Daiya is below," Marellon said, pointing down the tunnel. His hair was redder in this light, his skin pale gold. A golden nimbus shone around the edges of Luret's darker hair. The two seemed handsomer in the soft light; the dirt on their clothes was no longer visible. Impulsively, Lydee sent out a warm tendril of friendliness, but touched only their walls.

"I am ready," she said. "You may lead me to her."

"Daiya wishes to see you alone," Luret replied. Lydee stared down the tunnel uncertainly. "Just float down until you reach the bottom."

Lydee pressed her belt, launching herself into the tunnel. She dropped down past darkened walls; tentatively, she opened her link. She could feel the power in the mountain; her link hummed with it, feeding her. The tunnel grew lighter; the walls around her disappeared. Veils of blue and violet light fluttered near her; tiny lights twinkled in the air. Her boots clattered against a metal floor.

She was standing in the middle of a long, wide corridor. To her right, the corridor stretched so far that she could not see where it ended. She turned to her left and saw another long hallway. Several paces away, near a curved railing, a dark-haired woman sat; her head was bowed, and Lydee could not see her face.

She walked toward the woman, who made no sign that she was aware of Lydee's presence. As the girl came to the railing, she put her hands on it and peered down into the circle it enclosed. Gold and crystalline pillars were below her; she saw other railings, and more pillars below them. Earth's Mindcores had been hidden here for thousands of years; terror, and the wish to forget, had buried them.

"Are you going to keep staring?" a low voice said. Lydee went to the woman and sat down in front of her, trying not to show her apprehension.

Daiya AnraBrun's face was brown. Thin lines were etched around her eyes; two creases were on either side of her mouth. The skin of her neck was roughened, and her cream-colored tunic could not hide the slight sagging of her full breasts. Lydee, having seen only images of the woman as a girl, had not been prepared for the signs of age, even knowing what she did about Earth.

This was the one who had saved her from death. "Greetings," Lydee said softly, unable to bring herself to say the woman's name.

"Greetings. So you are Lydee."

The girl nodded. Daiya shook back her long, tangled hair, a mass of wiry curls that reached almost to her waist. "You look more like a person than I had expected—I can even see our father in your eyes. Don't try to touch my mind."

Lydee drew back, startled; the woman had sensed her intention before she herself was aware of it.

—Can you mindspeak?— Daiya's thoughts were clear and forceful.

—Yes, but I have had little practice—

—I do not know why your world's Mind gave you access to your powers without training you more thoroughly—

—There wasn't time— Lydee replied.

—You should have been given them sooner. I'll have to train you— Daiya paused. "How you can learn in a short time what takes a child years, I do not know," she continued aloud. Lydee put up her wall, although certain that the woman could penetrate it with little effort.

"Reiho told me to greet you for him," Lydee said, wishing that the woman would not frown so much.

"Reiho is dead."

"I meant the Reiho who has taken his place."

"I know whom you meant." Daiya's brown eyes were sad. "Reiho was my friend. He accepted me, while those here turned from me. I was afraid that his successor would not come here. I wanted to touch his mind to see if the Reiho I knew had left something of himself there. Well. You, at least, are here, sister."

Lydee nodded, feeling that Daiya was disappointed. "Why did you want one of us here?"

"You are needed. I can't explain it to you fully, but I felt that someone from your world should be here now. Maybe the Minds here are working through me— I don't know." She paused. "At first, it was only fear that made me call out to your world, fear of the wall that now surrounds us. Then Homesmind told me of Its discovery that your people could use the mind-powers we have. I knew then that if one of you returned here, the fear that my people have of your world might be dispelled—they would see that you are not really separate selves." She sighed. "I wish we could show that to other villages, but we are cut off, and the wall remains."

"The boy Marellon thinks I am useless."

"He is fearful. We don't know what will happen now. The Minds inside these mountains, and the other Minds in other regions of Earth, have been silent for many cycles of seasons. Once, They spoke to me and told me that we must awaken. Now it is They who sleep. They leave us power, but have abandoned us. They could break down the wall, but do not, and we can't summon enough strength to break it ourselves. We have tried, but our bodies weaken with the struggle.

A strong mind in a weak body is of no use, for body and mind are wedded."

"Perhaps I shouldn't stay," Lydee said. "There is nothing I can do."

Daiya's eyes narrowed. "You say that only because you're afraid. You don't know what you can or can't do, what your purpose is. You came here unwillingly, and now you want to run away." Lydee sensed the woman's icy anger. "You are one from our village and should remember that."

"That was long ago." Lydee, responding to the feelings she sensed, was growing angry herself. "You would have killed me."

Daiya laughed harshly. "I saved you."

"I'm a cometdweller now." The tenuous blue and violet veils fluttered, and she felt a breeze.

"Control yourself," Daiya said. "Do you want to raise the wind?" She leaned forward. "Training you will be difficult, and I can't take you to the village as you are. I know that the skydwellers don't share thoughts easily. You will have to let down your barriers and be willing to let us enter your mind. Think of us as unimportant creatures, or lower animals, if that makes it easier for you."

Lydee nodded, embarrassed by the words.

"It was hard for me, too," Daiya said more gently. "I have always sought solitude, and have kept apart from others. I understand you better than you think."

She waved a hand. "Go and rest. We'll begin tomorrow."

Lydee nodded as she stood up. Daiya's thoughts were hidden; she was already lost in contemplation. As Lydee walked back down the corridor, one last, gentle thought reached her.

—I am happy that you have a life, Lydee—

Lydee had been careful to keep her link closed during the night, afraid that her dreams might otherwise become all too real. She had awakened once to see the comet overhead, a streak against the sky, and then had dreamed that she was on a river, alone in the boat in which she had celebrated with her friends, drifting past a desolate, empty plain.

She sat outside the shuttle in the pink light of dawn, her feet dangling over the ledge, and nibbled at a protein cake. As long as she kept near the ship, the discomforts of Earth would not be too onerous; the synthesizer could provide her with food and water indefinitely, and she could tend to her bodily functions. Other supplies were tucked away in the craft's shelves in case the synthesizer failed; she had never heard of such a thing happening, but it was best to be safe. The ship had a small library, and she could always speak to Homesmind, so she would not lack entertainment, though she was unlikely to have time for such pursuits. Her spirits were lifting. If she was ever in great danger, her shuttle would carry her away from Earth.

She recalled her meeting with Daiya, trying to sort out her feelings. The woman was ignorant and much too direct, but her thoughts had conveyed strength and clarity, and Lydee had sensed her longing for wisdom.

Slowly, she opened her link. Power flowed through her; she took a deep breath. Someone was near her. She touched the mind gently and recognized Luret NenlaKal; she could, it seemed, distinguish one mind from another. Daiya's thoughts had felt hard and probing, while Luret's were more tentative. She let her thoughts expand and flow outward, strands of a web. Marellon BariWil was also nearby; his thoughts were grating and abrasive. She no longer sensed hostility, only doubt and suspicion. Shivering, she withdrew into herself, afraid that she might lose herself in the thoughts of others.

Luret crept around the front of the craft and sat down next to Lydee. "Did you sleep well?"

"Of course."

"Is it true that skydwellers do not have to sleep as we do? I see that it is." Luret blushed. "Your wall is thin, so I couldn't help seeing your answer. I'll touch only surface thoughts—it's hard for me to speak only with words."

"We have to sleep sometimes," Lydee replied. "We can go without it for long periods, but we have our limitations." She turned toward the other girl. "How do you control your dreams and keep them from disturbing others?"

"We keep our walls up during sleep. Small children have trouble doing that at first, so we must all shield ourselves. Their parents often have to cloak them so that they don't wake one another." Lydee felt a pang; Luret had seemed unhappy when she had mentioned children. "Sometimes people draw together and share a dream." This thought was also paining Luret.

Lydee was embarrassed, unwilling to explore the source of the other girl's sorrow. "I can sense," she said hastily, "that Marellon is near."

Luret raised an arm, pointing. "He's up there." The boy was sitting in a recess above them, gazing out at the desert. "He did not want to eat his morning meal near you—he felt how it bothered you yesterday." She could hide nothing from them. "He's trying to abide by your courtesy."

"Courtesy is simpler when you don't know what people are thinking. That's the point of it, I guess—to hide thoughts. We can link our thoughts, but most of us don't until we have known someone very well."

"But you can't know someone well without touching her thoughts, can you?"

Lydee shrugged. "It's a paradox, I suppose."

"It seems strange. I've touched the minds of everyone I know. But even we shield our thoughts at times. Many keep them from Daiya, as you know, and she must live apart from the village. It was a judgment passed on her, for many died when she revealed separateness to us."

"I don't know how that alone could have killed anyone."

"Everything they were taught seemed false, and they could not bear it. The mind can turn against itself." Luret shook her head. "I still think it's cruel. We've shared Daiya's knowledge, and we're all trapped behind that wall now, but many avoid her, and she has grown so used to her solitude that she may not be able to end it. Poor Daiya must live on a hill near our village, and though she can enter the village, she can't stay. Cerwen, father to Daiya's father Brun, was the one who decreed her punishment."

"Why did you seek her out, then?"

"My parents brought us to her at first, when we were children. Nenla, my mother, has been her friend since they were small, and my father Kal is Daiya's cousin." Luret smiled as a strand of her mind touched Lydee's. "Kal is your cousin, too—his father is brother to your mother."

Lydee tried not to show her indifference. Cousin, father, brother—they were only words designating a few shared genes, that was all.

Luret's smile faded. "Daiya told us stories of the world in the sky, and taught us mindcrafts. But we stopped going to her when we were older because others called us solitaries and saw dark places in our minds, voids filling with questions." Lydee saw an image in the other girl's mind; a dark young man with intense black eyes held up a hand, as if warding Luret off.

—Wiland— the Earthgirl thought as the image faded, and Lydee felt love mingled with pain. Luret raised her wall. "Daiya asked us to come here with her to meet you. She thought you might want to see someone your own age."

"That was kind."

"I know that she hoped another would be with you. Marellon and I must go now, so that she can train you."

"To your village?" Lydee asked.

Luret nodded.

"Isn't it a long way?"

"Two or three days, that is all."

"I could take you there in the shuttle and come back here much more quickly than that." She felt that she had to make the offer.

"You must not. You have to stay with Daiya for now, and the others are not yet ready to see you—you might find their thoughts hard to endure."

"At least let me give you some food and water."

Luret held up a hand. "You needn't do that. We'll pass streams and find game on the way." She sighed. "I wish you well, Lydee. Our village is troubled." She covered her green eyes for a moment. "I say to myself that no young one has died during our ordeals ever since Daiya showed us the truth of things, and that this may be a sign of some mercy, but I'm afraid a greater ordeal awaits all of us. It may be that we'll have to join God—the Merged One—and be at peace at last."

Lydee recoiled. The words were calm enough, but the girl's thoughts were of death.

Luret stood up. "Farewell, Lydee AnraBrun." She floated up toward Marellon, landing next to him on the mountainside. Lydee watched as the two began to climb.

The shuttle sat at the foot of the mountain. Lydee sat near it, feeling drained. She was not physically tired, but her mind lacked the will even to raise an arm. Daiya had been mindspeaking all morning, refusing to use words.

—Keep your wall up— Daiya was saying inside her now. —Leave only a small passage for my thoughts. While you do that, reach out to the Minds under the mountains and allow Their power to flow into you—

Lydee reached out; the stream strengthened her. She could now keep up her wall without strain while at the same time leaving it open just enough to grasp Daiya's surface thoughts. At first, the Earthwoman had formed her thoughts carefully, in distinct words; now Lydee could take in complete thoughts. Daiya seemed pleased; she had not expected even that much of Lydee in such a short period.

—Yes, you learn well enough— Daiya continued.

—But you still hold back too much. Do not fear. You'll overcome that, too, and it's wise to restrain yourself a bit— She gazed at Lydee pensively, obviously puzzling over a problem.

—You want to ask me something— Lydee thought.

Daiya nodded. —I'll find my answer another way— She waved a hand at the desert. —I want to see you fly without your belt. Can you do that?—

—I can try—

—Then take it off and let me see you fly—

Lydee tensed. —We never remove our belts unless we're resting. I've worn one for as long as I can remember—

—Do you need it here? Such tools are unnecessary. You have that suit of yours and your powers as well. Why do you need your belt?—

Lydee touched her waist. The belt not only gave her the power of flight, but also helped to pilot her; without it, she might make mistakes. She felt Daiya's scorn. Even if she fell, she could not be easily hurt; she was being too cautious. She took off the belt, dropping it to the ground as she stood up; the belt curled into a coil.

—Fly, Lydee—

She lifted herself cautiously, hovering for a moment before flying forward. Turning, she flew toward the mountains, rising until she was nearly as high as the peaks. She spun around and dropped toward Daiya more quickly. The wind shrieked; she squinted, grateful for the lenses that protected her eyes. She shot up suddenly. Daiya had shrunk; the shuttle was a turtle on the ground. Lydee hovered near a rocky cliff. She could peer over the mountains now, catching a glimpse of the green land on the other side.

—Do not fly too far from me— Daiya's thoughts were fainter.

—Shall I return?—

—Stay aloft for as long as you can—

Lydee dropped, brushing rock with her foot: steadying herself, she fell toward Daiya, twirling in the air as she circled the woman. She was free. She needed no belt, no tools; her mind, and the power that fed it, were enough.

She rose again, going so high that the mountains were soon only a ridge below her, a craggy gray-and-brown barrier separating yellow from green.

—Come back— Daiya whispered; her thoughts were harder to grasp. —Come back— The words were insistent. Lydee dived, arms out to slow her speed; the ground rushed toward her. Righting herself, she landed on her feet next to the shuttlecraft.

—You're still not tired— Daiya murmured.

—No—

—You could continue to fly—

—Yes— Lydee sat down, realizing that Daiya was disturbed.

—It is as I expected, Lydee. Your body, like Reiho's, is much stronger than mine. It is strengthened as you grow, isn't it?—

—Of course—

—I could not have stayed aloft as you did without strain. None of us could. Body and mind are one. We must work to strengthen ourselves physically, even doing tasks with our hands that we could do with our minds, so that we don't grow weak. Though we have the power of the Minds in the pillars to draw on, our bodies can fail us, and we cannot draw on it for difficult tasks without strain. Our old ones have weaker bodies, but since their minds have drawn close, their combined strength and greater skill in using their minds allow them to compensate for the weakness—

—And my body is stronger— Lydee thought, not sure for a moment if she was thinking her own thoughts or echoing Daiya's. —That means I can use more power. It means my mind is stronger— She lifted herself from the ground again.

—Foolish girl— Daiya's cold thoughts doused her joy; she landed and sat down again. —Unchecked powers can be as dangerous as weak ones. And keep this in mind: We have more experience than you. We have each been tested in an ordeal, and those who did not measure up died—

Daiya's thoughts were sobering. Homesmind had told Lydee about the ordeal every young person on

Earth had to undergo. Boys and girls were sent in small groups away from their villages, deprived of mental contact with anyone except one another. Isolated from the Net of a village for the first time in their lives, their terror became so great that many could not fight it and gave up their lives. Lydee could understand such fear now, away from Home. She would never be able to endure it if she lost her own link with Homesmind and her world.

—You understand— Daiya said, picking up Lydee's thoughts.

Do not fear, Homesmind whispered consolingly.

Lydee shared some of her food with Daiya, then spent the afternoon learning to lift objects with her mind, beginning with rocks and ending with the shuttle, which she was able to hold in the air for several minutes. Daiya was clearly impressed, but Lydee knew how much she still had to learn.

She offered more food to Daiya that evening as the sky grew purple and the desert air cooled. Daiya seemed tired; she had been forced to restrain Lydee several times, binding her thoughts when the girl grew too daring.

—You will have to be careful near the village— Daiya thought as she ate. —You're not used to touching many minds—

Lydee felt apprehensive.

—I'll help you— Daiya continued. —You will not have to feel their thoughts all at once. Our sister Silla may come to us, for she's curious about you in spite of herself, and her partner Harel KaniDekel is my friend— A wall was suddenly around Daiya's mind, and Lydee could not sense the woman's feelings.

They finished their meal. Daiya shivered in the mountains' shadow, then warmed the air around her. Lydee got up, walking east until she came to the invisible barrier, and began to probe it with her mind. Even her thoughts could not penetrate it. She pushed; the barrier was unyielding.

Daiya came to her side. —This wall is not only of thought— she said. —If it were, we could close our minds to it, and be able to walk through it. But those who hold it there have made it a physical barrier as well—

—A force field— Lydee thought. —Even my ship sensed it when I approached, and could not have flown through it but had to drop inside of it— She paused. —In the shuttle, I could fly over it and land on the other side—

—That would be unwise. You would be exposed to all the minds outside and might be killed. Your body is strong, but your mind can still be crushed. The wall seals us off, but it also protects us— Daiya sent out a cold wave of fear. —When I think of how many people must be holding it there, I'm afraid. Every mind on

Earth must be contributing its force to the wall—

—Will it stay there forever, then?—

—We can't know. Perhaps they are merely guarding themselves from us, and will allow us to live out our lives behind it until we have died out. They may not have to wait long. My village has been afflicted for several cycles. Perhaps I should have called out for help sooner, but I thought we would overcome our incapacities—

Lydee could taste the bitterness in Daiya's thoughts. —What do you mean?—

Her sister's shield was up. —You will see soon enough— Daiya turned back toward the shuttle, glaring at the mountains. —And still the Minds do not speak to me. They promised my people a way to live with the knowledge Reiho and I brought to my village. Now They will bring us only death—

Daiya strode toward the shuttle as Lydee hurried after her. —There is another way— she said. —It might be why I was sent here. We could build a home for you in space and take your people there—

—We can't live as you do—

—Homesmind would help— Lydee clung to her notion, which now seemed so obvious an answer.

Daiya shook her head. —You don't know us. This is our home; we would die away from it. I saw that when Reiho showed me your world—

—But yours doesn't have to be like ours—

Daiya stopped and faced her. —You say this only because it would give you a way to flee— Lydee looked down, knowing the woman was right. —You would go back and you would find that the other skydwellers care little about what happens to us. Few would help you— Lydee stepped back, startled. —Oh, yes. You forget that I can see your thoughts clearly. I know how we are regarded by skydwellers. You would run away and console yourself by thinking you had done what you could—

"I am trying to help," Lydee said aloud, afraid that if she mindspoke, her words would prickle with anger. "You could live on a world so like Earth that you would forget this place. You could strengthen your bodies and have long lives. Why stay?"

—There are the other villages to consider—

"Why do you care so much about them when they only want to wall you in?"

—They would be left in ignorance. They would never learn of the Minds in the pillars, and that it was our ancestors who built Them. They would never understand that separate selves can be given powers, too. It would be evil to separate ourselves from them. Separateness of that kind leads to hatred and death. Reiho taught me that, even if some of his own people have yet to learn it— She looked up at the comet. —It seems he's forgotten it too—

Lydee wanted to comfort her, but the emotional

exchange had overwhelmed her. Raising her wall, she withdrew into herself.

Lydee stretched, then looked out through her shuttle's dome. The sun was already peeking over the distant horizon.

Daiya was still sleeping, curled up on the ground outside. Lydee had offered her a place inside the shuttle, but Daiya had refused it; she had at last forced the Earthwoman to accept a blanket. The silvery fabric wrinkled as Daiya began to stir.

A panel in front of Lydee lit up. Stunned, she stared at the flickering symbols; another shuttle was near. Reiho, she thought wildly.

Yes, Homesmind said. *Reiho is going to join you after all.* Homesmind's voice was subdued.

"He's overcome his fear, then."

His fear is still with him, Lydee. He requested that I dull it for him, but I cannot do too much without slowing his reflexes. That wouldn't matter here, but there his mind must be sharp and aware. You will have to be patient with him, and watch out for him with Daiya's help.

Her joy faded. Her visit would be difficult enough; how could she be responsible for Reiho? Maybe, she thought, he shouldn't have come.

Perhaps not. Homesmind replied, answering her thoughts. *But his shame at allowing you to travel to*

Earth by yourself became greater than his fear. He must live with himself in times to come. I had to let him go.

She clasped her hands together; the symbols before her blurred.

Do not fear. I'll watch over both of you.

That, she thought resentfully, had not helped Reiho before. She pressed her lips together; she was being unfair. Homesmind had felt pain at Reiho's death; It was now trying to make up for Its own failure.

The shuttle door opened; she jumped out of the craft. Daiya was standing, clutching at the blanket, looking up at the sky as the dark speck above grew larger.

—Reiho— she said, picking up Lydee's thoughts.

The vehicle dropped toward them; its runners were now visible. It landed a few paces away, raising small clouds of dust. Daiya dropped the silver blanket and ran toward Lydee; her thoughts were stormy, clouds of apprehension dimming the glow of anticipation inside her. "Reiho," she said aloud.

The man stepped from his ship and looked around fearfully. Lydee rushed toward him, then halted, afraid she might overwhelm him with her welcome. "You came after all," she said as calmly as she could.

"I was afraid I'd turn back. Every moment of the journey, I was afraid I wouldn't be able to go on." He took her hands. "I'm all right. I don't know how much help I'll be—I'm still afraid."

He was gazing past her at Daiya, who was hanging

back. Lydee could not read her mind. She and Reiho had been speaking in their own language, and he had managed somehow to shield his thoughts, but his weak wall was beginning to crumble, and she could sense his agitation. "Close your link," she said. "You mustn't let too much power flow in too quickly."

"Daiya," he said.

The woman walked toward him and stopped a few paces away. "You are not the same," she murmured in her own tongue. "Your soul is not that of the Reiho I knew. I see your earlier self, and then a break, and then another's life. You remember me, but I am only someone you dreamed. Your curiosity is no longer a bright flame but an ember, while your fear has become a claw poised to tear at you. You are not the one I knew, and yet I see part of him inside you."

Reiho was struggling to shield his thoughts. Lydee felt Daiya's mind reach out to calm him; the air around him grew cooler. His face changed, looking like a boy's for a moment. "I can touch your mind, and you can hear my thoughts, but I won't mindspeak without your consent." Daiya paused. "Do not fear me, Reiho."

He stretched out an arm tentatively. Daiya touched his fingers, then withdrew her hand. "We have much to do," she said briskly. "Now I must teach mindcraft to you as well as to my sister, and I don't know how much time will be granted to us." She glanced toward the invisible barrier. "Let us begin."

6

The wren dipped its curved beak, bowing, then hopped toward Lydee. She held it with her mind. It fluttered up and perched on her outstretched arm; she let it go.

The small brown bird flew out toward the invisible wall. A strand of her mind caught it, directing it away from the barrier. It darted back to the mountain, disappearing behind a boulder.

She was sitting on a rocky shelf. Below her, near the shuttles, Reiho sat with Daiya, lifting dirt and sand with his mind and shaping it into figures. One pillar of dirt became the outline of a man, then turned into a small mound as Reiho released it.

They had been in the desert for nearly two weeks, honing their mental skills. Reiho had struggled at first with the unfamiliar abilities; because he was older than Lydee, he had been more set in his ways, more hesitant to try his powers. Lydee, on the other hand, had needed to develop more caution; there were still times when she would show off, keeping her shuttle in the air for hours at a time while she hovered near it, testing the limits of her body and mind. They could make a game of their mindpowers now, but she did not know how well they would handle a meeting with the village. Even Daiya's gentle probing often seemed intrusive.

Homesmind rarely spoke to them. It was still observing Earth through her eyes and Reiho's, but she was beginning to feel isolated both from It and from the comet. The longer she stayed here, the harder it would be to return.

Reiho and Daiya were now communing silently. Lydee had glimpsed how he saw the woman; when Reiho gazed at Daiya, her face was smoother and her body more taut, for he saw the girl his former self had known, and Daiya often saw him as a boy. Lydee, unwilling to disturb the illusion their minds created, occasionally saw them that way, too. Deep currents flowed between the two that even they seemed unwilling to acknowledge. Reiho would always shy away from strong feelings, and Daiya still held part of herself back.

Daiya had told them of her hopes for Earth, of how those born as solitaries might be saved and taught. She would need the cometdwellers' help then, for the weak ones would need implants to strengthen their minds. Lydee frowned. Homesmind could provide the tools for that work; surely she and Reiho would have left Earth by then. She was thinking too far ahead; the wall around them still held.

She stood up, lifted herself, and flew toward the wall, soaring easily through the warm air. Daiya was concentrating on Reiho's thoughts; Lydee would be free to attempt what she had been wanting to try. Landing in front of the barrier, she steadied herself, then aimed her thoughts.

The wall remained, as she had expected. She summoned more power, directing it at a space near her head, pushing against the field. Her mind hummed; dirt lifted around her feet. She called on all her strength; pain shot through her temples, almost disabling her.

A point glowed on the wall, becoming a small circle. Already she was growing weak from the effort. The glow expanded; a bit of the wall suddenly gave way.

A gust of wind tore at her ankles. She fell to the ground and lay on her back, unable to move, waiting for her strength to return.

A shadow fell across her face. Daiya was standing over her, Reiho at her side. —What are you doing?—

"I did it." Lydee sat up slowly, too exhausted to mindspeak. "I moved the wall a little, I could feel it. It took all my strength, but I almost tore a hole in it."

—You foolish girl— Daiya dragged her to her feet. Lydee staggered, almost too weak to stand. —Do you want to draw their wrath?—

"I've shown that the wall can be breached."

—I see that you're proud of your great strength, but you cannot tear it down alone—

"Others could help me. Are you content to live behind it forever?"

—Those outside may feel safe from us now— Daiya replied, —but they won't if you assault the wall. They will only make it stronger—

—They cannot keep it up indefinitely— Reiho said.

Daiya shook her head. —I don't know. They must be drawing on most of their strength now, and that will weary them. But there are many of them. Some will sustain it while others rest—

—Perhaps you should do something besides wait— Lydee thought; she was recovering her strength. —We could add our minds to yours, and then—

—Break the wall?— Daiya's thoughts stung. —And then what? Are you willing to face death? Do you want Reiho to face it again?—

Lydee spun around and strode toward the shuttles. Daiya's passivity was beginning to annoy her. —You'll endanger us— Daiya continued as she came up to the girl's side. —Your carelessness will bring harm. Reiho's fear will seize him, and you'll be free to run away in your craft while we'll be left to face the consequences of your actions. And you might not get away. You might be torn from the sky—

—Stop!— Lydee cried out as she turned. Daiya tensed; Reiho, behind her, looked pained. She had given the word too much force. That was what came of sharing thoughts, Lydee said to herself; too many strong feelings were released, however much she struggled for control.

—Reiho overcame his fear to come here— she continued. —You should not remind him of his terrors. And I am trying to help you—

Daiya was silent for a moment; her mind's tendrils curled inward. —You are right— she said at last. —But heed me. You have both learned quickly, but this is my world, and you must take my advice. You, Lydee, are still a child. Don't feel so resentful, I'm only stating a fact. You must let me guide you—

Lydee did not reply. Reiho was shielding his thoughts.

—Perhaps you have shown me something important— Daiya said more gently. —If a hole can be torn in that wall, we may find a way to destroy it. But until we know what those outside will do, it is wiser not to act—

—But we're cut off from their thoughts— Lydee said. —You can't know what they're planning—

—Be patient. Your power can injure those you are trying to help— Daiya was directing her thoughts only to Lydee as Reiho climbed into the craft to fetch food.

—Reiho was not the only one who died when I was trying to protect him long ago. Many in my village died, struck down by their despair when they saw that the world was not what they believed it to be. I'll carry that guilt for the rest of my life. You would not want to have that burden—

Lydee sat down. Reiho came to her and handed her some fruit; she ate without tasting it. He was nibbling at his own food, as if forcing himself to eat. The wind sang mournfully; she caught the icy thoughts of a lizard, so rooted to instinct that they were hardly thoughts at all.

—We have worked here long enough— Daiya said as she ate. —We must go to the village now—

Reiho seemed pained. "I can't," he said aloud.

Daiya glanced at him. "What do you mean?" she asked. "Open your mind and let me see. You knew we would have to go there."

"You know what I mean without seeing my thoughts. I've come this far, but I'm not ready for that."

"Am I to leave you here? Or are you going to go back to the sky?"

"Please try to understand. My former self died there, and I'm still afraid to face it."

"The village won't harm you now."

"They killed my former self."

"What are you going to do, then?" Daiya was restraining herself; Lydee could feel the woman's urge to rip at Reiho's mental wall.

"I can come with you part of the way. You'll still be able to send your thoughts out to me. I need time to overcome this last vestige of my fear—surely you can see that. I must prepare myself."

—Very well— Daiya said with her mind. —But if you cannot grow braver in a little while, it might be best if you left Earth entirely. My people can't trust you if you don't trust them— The woman was trying to cloak her disappointment with compassion.

Lydee swallowed. She would see the place where she might have lived and the people who had turned her away.

The shuttle landed at the bottom of a hill. Daiya climbed out, glancing skeptically at the craft; she still distrusted the vehicle and had kept her eyes closed during most of the journey, opening them only when they were near the village.

Lydee hung back, checked her pack, then pulled at the sleeves of her brown shirt. Daiya had insisted that she wear a shirt and pants over her silver suit, telling Lydee that the clothes would make her look more human. She put on her pack and climbed out.

To the east, the mountains jutted toward the sky. Reiho was near the foothills, too far away to be seen; she began to wish she had stayed with him. Daiya motioned to her; Lydee followed the woman up the hill.

Daiya's hut, made of mud bricks, was at the top of

the slope in a grove of trees. As Lydee neared it, she could glimpse the village beyond. A grassy expanse separated the village from the hill; she could now imagine, even without touching Daiya's thoughts, how cruel her exile must have been. She had lived here on this hill, able to watch the community without being able to share in its life except as a visitor, knowing that no other village would give her a home. Even absolute solitude might have been easier to bear.

The village's huts stood in concentric circles surrounding an open space. Several people had gathered in the space; she thought she saw a few of them glance toward the hill. Others were on the riverbank, dipping buckets into the water. Ditches ran from the river to the fields bordering the town; villagers were laboring among the wheat and corn. Lydee cautiously let out a tendril, wary of being swamped by hundreds of thoughts, but the village remained silent. The Earth-folk had apparently decided to shield themselves from her, and she sensed only the weaker, more indirect thoughts of their hens, pigs, dogs, and cats.

—Don't expect them to reach out to you right away— Daiya thought. Lydee took off her pack, and Daiya dropped it inside the doorway of her hut. —I must go into the village now. You'll be all right here, won't you?—

Lydee nodded.

—Marellon and Luret will stay here for the night,

outside my hut, so you won't be alone. I must speak with our Merging Selves— She turned and walked down the slope toward the village.

The Merging Selves. Lydee's mind curled tightly around that thought. The Merging Selves were the older villagers, people who mingled their thoughts so freely that at times they were almost one mind. She wondered how a person could endure such a loss of the self. It seemed a kind of death, yet all Earthpeople aspired to such a state and wanted to live long enough to become Merging Selves.

Lydee sat down, feeling disappointed. She had expected more of a reception; she was, after all, from another world, a transformed child of the village, yet they still shunned her. They might be hoping she would leave.

She turned toward the doorway, peering inside the hut. The dim light revealed blackened bits of wood inside a circle of stones in the center of the dirt floor. There were openings between the walls and the grass roof, shelves of earthen pots and bowls, and a reed mat. Even with her own supplies, she was likely to be uncomfortable at best; Daiya was expecting her to stay in the hut rather than in the shuttle, presumably to demonstrate to the village how like them she was.

I can't stay here, she thought. The village seemed to alter as she gazed at it, becoming shabby and mean. The bright afternoon sun dimmed, the river became brown and muddy, the fields overgrown. Daiya, striding away below, was an aging, worn woman too stubborn to give up her hard life for the ease the cometdwellers could offer. Lydee shook her head. Her mind shaped what she saw here; she wondered if she could actually see the village as it really was.

An invisible hand touched her shoulder. She tensed. A glow had appeared inside the hut. Standing, she crept through the doorway, then wondered if she should call for help. Another mind was touching hers; she put up her wall.

Her mental barrier suddenly shattered into shards of light.

Lydee gasped, staggering back against a wall. The glow brightened; her mind was humming with voices. She tried to run, but her legs would not move.

The brightness dimmed. A golden-haired woman in a long, blue robe stood before her. Lydee struggled; invisible arms were holding her.

"Who are you?" she cried, forgetting to speak with her mind. —Who are you?— she said again.

The woman smiled, holding out a hand. Lydee reached for her; her hand passed through the woman's arm. She pulled back. —Are you from the village? Are you someone's image sent to greet me?—

—I am not— The thought was strong; Lydee's link trembled.

—Then you're from another village— That would

mean that the barrier had been breached; she shook
with fear.

—I am not—

—Who are you, then?—

Inside her, Homesmind whispered, *I know what you
are.*

—I am one who once lived— the woman replied.
—My body is now dust. I speak to you first, because
you are from another place. Prepare yourself. I see a
time approaching when change will at last come to
this village and to those outside it, and you are a tool
of that change. Strengthen yourself. Purge yourself of
anger, no matter what you may see. Open your mind
to compassion and understanding, for they may be the
weapons you will need. Remember that a mind striking
out in rage will wound itself as well as its target. Forget
your fear—

I know what you are, Homesmind said again.

—Silence, young Mind. Her ordeal approaches, and
she must go to her fate without Your aid— The woman
faded, then flickered out.

Lydee crumpled to the dirt floor. —Homesmind—

There was no answer.

"Homesmind!" Her channel would not open; something was wrong with her link. "Homesmind!" She was
cut off from the comet, unable to transmit; she wondered if Homesmind could still hear her.

—It will observe— the woman's voice said inside

her. —But It cannot answer your call. You must rely on yourself—

"Restore my link!"

—You have your mindpowers. You do not need anything else—

"Don't leave me like this!" She waited, expecting to hear the voice again, but her mind was silent now. Leaning over, she held her stomach, afraid she would be sick. An ordeal, the woman had said. She would never be able to endure it. "Homesmind," she whispered.

She forced herself to sit up. The woman had told her that her body was dust; did that mean she had been speaking to a ghost? She shook her head. Daiya's people had many odd beliefs, but even they knew that one could not summon the dead.

She got to her feet and hurried outside, afraid to stay inside the hut. Luret and Marellon were climbing up the hill. She clenched her teeth and buttressed the shield around her thoughts, afraid to let the two see them.

"You look more human," Marellon said, gazing at her clothes as he dropped a rolled-up mat. "Have you learned how to mindspeak properly?"

"I can mindspeak."

"Then please do so."

—You are disturbed— Luret said, sitting down on her own mat. —You can't hide that. Something has happened to you—

Lydee sank to the ground. Marellon sprawled in the grass, gazing at her with expressionless brown eyes; she could sense no sympathy from him.

—I must tell someone— Lydee said. —A woman appeared to me. She took form inside the hut, but she was an image, not a body. She wasn't one of you and she wasn't one of my people, either—

—Show us— Luret said gently.

Lydee opened her mind, reluctantly allowing the two to see what she had experienced while masking her own reactions. Luret's green eyes widened in surprise as she grasped the thoughts: Marellon scowled. They were obviously as puzzled by the woman's appearance as she was.

—What can it mean?— Luret asked.

Lydee sighed. —I was expecting you to tell me—

—I have never heard of such a thing—

—It's a delusion— Marellon thought. —She is not one of us and not from another village, and it's clear she's not from your world, either. So you imagined her and thought you saw her, but you saw only your mind's imaginings—

—You're wrong— Lydee responded. —Homesmind, the Mind of my world, sensed her as well. It said that It knew what she was—

—But It didn't tell you— the boy said.

—It didn't have a chance—

—No. You imagined it all. A mind can turn against itself, fall prey to illusion. And think of what she said, that she was appearing to you first. You think too much of yourself, skydweller. You come here for a short time and already you believe that you have some ability we don't, and now your mind is feeding your pride—

—Marellon— Luret was trying to calm the boy, dulling the sharp edges of his thoughts.

Maybe it's true, Lydee thought to herself. The apparition had seemed real enough, but her mind could create many illusions here. "No," she said aloud, denying that. "I can't speak to Homesmind. I could not have closed that channel by myself."

—You're mad— Marellon said. —Your mind is fighting itself, and you don't even see it. You're trying to find enough courage to stay, which is why you had your vision, but at the same time you long to flee, and forget us—

"I'm cut off from my world!" she cried.

—You can always go back—

—Stop it, Marellon— Luret protested. Lydee jumped to her feet. —There may be something important in all this. Lydee may have seen something new—

"I don't care if I have," Lydee said harshly. "You can stay in your filthy little village. I'm leaving." She started down the hill toward her shuttle.

The craft suddenly rose in the air. She lifted a hand to her lips as the vehicle soared overhead, then fled from Earth, rushing up to the pink-edged evening clouds. "Come back!"

The shuttle was gone.

Marellon's mouth was open. Luret slouched forward, wrapping her arms around herself.

"Reiho," Lydee murmured. "I must go to Reiho." She launched herself from the slope and flew toward the distant foothills, afraid of what she might find.

Reiho's craft sat near a brook; he was inside, curled up on a seat, unmoving. Lydee had been calling to him through her link as she flew, but he had not answered. He's dead, she thought; his fear's crushed him.

She leaned against the ship; her flight had drained her. Gathering her strength, she pressed the door. It slid open and she climbed inside clumsily.

"Reiho."

His eyes shot open; his hands flew up, as if he was warding off a blow.

"Reiho."

"A man spoke to me." His voice was hoarse. "He appeared inside the shuttle, and said I must prepare myself. I'm cut off from Homesmind, Lydee."

"So am I."

He groaned, covering his face. "Then we're lost."

"We'll leave now, in your ship."

"We can't. I tried. It won't take off."

She clasped her hands together. "My shuttle's gone, Reiho."

"Then we're trapped."

She wanted to scream. "Homesmind will send help."

"What if It can't?"

She sat down next to him, huddling against the seat. They were silent for a long time, walled inside themselves. At last she said, "Homesmind said It knew who the woman was. A woman appeared to me, you see, and told me to prepare for an ordeal." She shivered at the word, which she had to say in Earth's tongue; the same word in her own language seemed too muted. "It said It knew."

"I think I know what she was, and what the man was, too."

"What, then?"

He sat up slowly. "I think Earth's Mindcores must have sent the images to us."

She had not thought of that; now it seemed an obvious possibility.

"Consider," he continued. "They might be images of people from Earth's past. The man told me his body was dust. The Minds might have presented what They can remember of him, as Homesmind can do with those who once lived on the comet. The Minds may have finally broken Their silence."

"But Daiya has been waiting for Them to speak. Why didn't They speak to her?"

"Maybe They will now."

She clutched at his hand. "Reiho, what will we do?"

"We're Their prisoners now. I'm afraid—" His voice broke. "I'm afraid," he said more softly, "that we'll have to do whatever They want us to do."

7

Reiho was kneeling by the brook. He dipped a cupped hand into the water, peered at the liquid, then sipped it tentatively.

Lydee shuddered. She sat in the shuttle's open doorway, afraid to move any farther. She had spent part of the morning trying to communicate with Homesmind through the shuttle before admitting it was hopeless.

"This water seems clean enough," Reiho said. "I analyzed it before, and it's relatively uncontaminated. We could probably drink the village's water, too. I don't know about the food. I suppose we could get along on vegetables and fruit, but we might get a little sick until our digestion adjusts to it."

Lydee made a face. He was assuming that they might

lose his shuttle as well. Eating dirty fruit and vegetables would be bad enough; she would never be able to tolerate meat.

Reiho stood up. "Of course, we have our mind-powers. The people here can heal themselves of many ailments, so maybe we won't get too sick."

"Don't talk that way," she said. Although they were not using mindspeech, undercurrents of thought were still passing between them. Reiho's cold and dark despair was a strand braided with her brighter, warmer tendrils of anger and fear. "I'm not leaving the shuttle. We can stay here. At least the synthesizer still works."

"You'll have to leave it sometime," he said mildly. "For one thing, you'll have to go back to the village."

"I'm not going back."

"Lydee, think. Whatever happens, it's clear that we're trapped here until we do whatever we're supposed to do."

"We don't even know what that is."

"Well, we'll probably find out soon."

"You're so calm about it all."

"You know that's not true. You can touch my thoughts and see that."

She sighed. She was only a tool to be used by some intelligence she could not fully understand. Homesmind, Who had raised her and taught her, had probably viewed her from the same perspective as she had viewed microbes when she was learning biology. The

people of the Wanderer were, to Homesmind, varia-
tions of genetic materials, new combinations of qualities; It determined their characteristics while allowing
for novelty and originality. She had sensed the Mindcore's perspective through her link. It knew their thoughts
and watched them live and die while It gathered their
knowledge and experience; It had come to surpass
them. It might even have been manipulating the cometdwellers for eons toward some distant end only It could
glimpse. Earth's Minds were still more fearsome, for
They had apparently surpassed Homesmind.

"We might not ever get back," she said.

"I know." He seemed resigned. "I suppose I always
knew I'd have to come back here after Homesmind
restored me, that I'd have to see where I died. It was
meant to be."

"Stop it. You're sounding like a superstitious Earthman now."

He walked over to her, resting his hands on the ship
as he gazed up at her face. "You have to go back to
Daiya."

"I won't go."

"You have to go. If you don't, she'll call out to you,
or send someone for you. I'll go with you, Lydee. It's
time I forced myself to face the village." He paused.
"Or maybe I'm just afraid of staying here alone."

"We can't leave the shuttle. We'll die without it."

He laughed mirthlessly. "You forget—we can move

it with our minds. We don't have the strength to take it away from Earth, but we ought to be able to get as far as the village."

She moved aside as he climbed into the craft. The door slid shut as they settled into their seats.

"Are you ready?" Reiho asked. "This is going to be exhausting work."

She nodded. His fear had become a hard, solid mass at the core of his mind; for a moment, she wondered if she was seeing his fear or her own.

She gripped the arms of her seat, allowing energy to flow into her. The shuttle lifted slightly and began to move in the village's direction, its runners brushing the grass.

Lydee climbed toward Daiya's hut, tired by her journey. Even with their combined efforts, she and Reiho had been forced to rest from time to time, and it had taken them most of the day to reach Daiya's hill. Several villagers had stared at them as they passed the fields, wondering at their desperate need for the vessel and their foolishness in draining themselves of strength to move it there.

Reiho had decided to remain inside the shuttle, below the hill. She had read his thoughts and knew that his fear of the village was not entirely gone. Now she worried about leaving him alone. Moving the shuttle had not left him much time to think about his fears;

alone, with little to do, he would have all too much time to consider his predicament.

Daiya was sitting outside her hut. A younger, brown-skinned woman with black hair was with her. Lydee could sense the woman's dislike and raised her mental shield.

Daiya lifted a hand in greeting. —You shouldn't have run away— she said, —but I understand why you did. Marellon and Luret showed me what happened to you. You have had a vision—

—I believe the Minds here spoke to me— Lydee said.

Daiya frowned; the other woman drew her brows together. —It could not have been the Minds— Daiya said. —They do not speak in that way, sending such images. At least They never did before—

—I don't know what else it could have been—

"So you know more about what happens here than we do, who have lived here all our lives." The other woman had a low, husky voice; her words were loud and sharp.

—Whatever it was— Daiya thought, —it was a sign. I see that it has brought Reiho here as well—

—He had his own vision. A man spoke to him—

"So now we'll have two of them inflicted upon us," the younger woman said.

—I can mindspeak— Lydee said.

"I won't mindspeak to you. I don't want to have your

thoughts poison me. I came here to see you with my eyes and hear you with my ears, but I won't touch your mind. If you see my thoughts, you will twist them and try to deceive me."

"I've come here to help," Lydee said aloud.

"And exactly what are you going to do?" The woman showed her teeth in a grim smile. "I see that you don't know. This is your fault, Daiya. You called to them and brought them here."

"Who are you?" Lydee burst out.

"I am Silla AnraBrun."

Lydee paused in the middle of removing the pack she was carrying, and let it slide from her shoulders as she sat down. "Then you are my other sister."

"I am Daiya's sister, not yours, and that is enough of a burden."

"You're Lydee's sister too," Daiya said.

"You should not be here, skydweller." Silla turned toward Daiya. "Tell her what you've done to us, with your separateness and your talk of how the world must pass into a new state and shed old ways. Tell her how long I've lived with my partner, and how no children come to us." She glared at Lydee. "And I'm not the only one so cursed. There has been no child born here in almost ten cycles of the seasons. Has she told you that?"

Lydee glanced at Daiya uncertainly.

"It's true," Silla went on. "Some were born after our

time of troubles, while we wrestled with the cursed knowledge Daiya had shown to us, but now there are none. That is a sign, a sign that we are condemned. And now two skydwellers are here. The last time that happened, many died. Now we will all die and leave no children to remember us and maintain our Net."

Lydee stared past Silla at the village below, recalling Luret's sorrow at the mention of children. A man was crossing the meadow, striding toward the hill; she wondered if another villager was coming to berate her.

"It may not mean that," Lydee said tentatively, wanting to console the angry woman somehow. "We have few children on the comet, but that only means we have no place for them at this time. When it is necessary, Homesmind will—"

"I don't care about your customs," Silla muttered. "I should have had at least two children by now, and I have none, and others have none. We'll die out."

—You know why you have none— Daiya thought, making her words clear and distinct. —Your anger and fear keep you from conceiving. Rid yourself of poisonous thoughts, and you'll have your children—

Silla narrowed her eyes. —That is not the reason for my failure— Lydee tensed; Silla's thoughts were cold and pointed. —You still have a spell on my partner Harel. You loved him once, and he loved you. Foolishly I thought that was in the past, but even now, he still sees you when he looks at me—

—You know that's not true— Daiya said sadly.

—Do you think I can't touch his mind? He doesn't see me, sister. He sees what you might have been if you hadn't grown separate from us— Silla straightened, throwing her shoulders back. —Even now, he approaches. He'll use any excuse to be near you— Lydee turned her head: the man was climbing the hill toward them.

—He rejected me, Silla— Daiya thought. —It was not I who turned him away. I can touch Harel's mind, too. He feels only friendship. The rest was lost long ago—

—He hides part of himself from me, and has secret thoughts—

—If you looked inside him with love instead of jealousy and suspicion, you would see that it is you he cares for. He would not hide part of himself from you then—

Silla's wall went up as the man came near; Lydee watched him as she put up her own wall again. The man had auburn hair and a short beard; he lifted his hand. Daiya's face was composed as she greeted him; Lydee could not read her thoughts.

"Why are you here?" Silla asked without facing him.

"I wanted to see the skydweller who is your sister." Silla grimaced as the man gazed at Lydee with kind, blue eyes. "Welcome, young one. I see that you have the look of Daiya on your face."

"You will see Daiya in anything," Silla said harshly.

A look of pain crossed the man's face as he knelt next to his partner, putting a hand on her shoulder. "I am Harel KaniDekel," he said to Lydee. "I wanted you to know that some of us don't bear you ill will."

Lydee nodded.

"I see," Silla said. "You have come here to make a fool of me. But there are more who feel as I do." A wave flowed out from the young woman; the village rippled as if the air itself had been distorted. Lydee flinched under the mental blow and buttressed her shield.

"No," Harel said, restraining his partner's mind.

"You should have gone far away," Silla shouted at Daiya. "You thought the Minds under the mountains would save us, but even now They are planning our doom. They could have torn down the wall around us, yet it remains." She rose; Harel also stood, gripping her hand. "Go back to your world, skydweller. You are no sister of mine."

"I can't go back," Lydee replied.

"Then you will die here, too." Silla shook off Harel's hand, turned, and strode down the hill.

Harel held out his arms. "I am sorry," he said before following his partner. Daiya watched him leave, her face stiff; Lydee sensed her longing before the Earthwoman suppressed it.

"You should have told me these things," Lydee said.

"You made me think that those in the village would come to accept me."

"They don't all feel as Silla does. Harel doesn't. My friend Nenla and my cousin Kal do not."

"You forget that I can touch your mind. I see that many do."

Daiya sighed. —I see that you can no longer speak to Homesmind— she thought. —I know how that pains you. I wish I could help you, but I can't hear It, either. It spoke to me through a channel the Minds here created for It, but that passage is also closed. That's why I'm beginning to believe that the Minds here have in fact spoken to you—

—Maybe not— Lydee responded. —Those outside the barrier might have closed it, and sent an image to deceive me—

—They probably don't know you're here, or what you are. They cannot touch your thoughts, and could not know how to shut off the channel to Homesmind, and they could not act without removing the wall around us. If they had opened the wall, the Merging Selves would have sensed it, and all of the village would have known— Daiya's reasoning seemed sound, but her thoughts lacked force.

—You must be right— Lydee said, trying to feel confident.

—I believed that the Minds under the mountains wanted what was best for us. But perhaps They want only to rule, and don't care what damage Their power causes—

—They cannot be so cruel— Lydee objected.

—They may not think of it as cruelty. They watched many die here and did nothing to stop it. Perhaps They could not, or maybe They simply chose not to act— Daiya walled in her thoughts, but her eyes betrayed her sorrow.

"Reiho?" Lydee said.

He was squatting in the shuttle's open door, outlined by its light. Even at night, Earth was awake; an owl was soaring over the meadow below, searching for prey. Lydee tore herself away from the predator's instinctual thoughts.

"Daiya will give you a place in her hut to sleep," Lydee murmured. "She says we should try to follow village ways as much as possible, so that others will grow to trust us."

"There's a more practical reason for doing so. We may have to live that way indefinitely." Reiho stood up swiftly, rummaged among the shelves and dispenser inside, then threw out two large packs. "We may as well take some supplies with us." He pulled a black tunic over his head, then put on a pair of dark pants; except for his silver boots, he might almost have passed as a villager.

As he jumped to the ground, the craft's door slid

shut and its light went out. They began to climb the hill; Reiho sneaked glances at the vehicle, as though expecting it to disappear. Its darkened dome bore a bright slash, a reflection of the comet overhead. We'll get away, Lydee thought. Even now Homesmind was probably trying to find a way to reach them.

She took Reiho's hand as they entered the hut. Daiya was stirring the dying embers of her fire, huddling over it as if performing a rite. Lydee had put a mattress in one corner earlier; she stretched out on it, waiting for Reiho to put away their provisions.

He lay down beside her. She felt his mental shield enclose his thoughts as he drifted off to sleep. Curling up on her left side, Lydee was about to doze off when she became aware of Daiya's murmurings.

—Please help us— Daiya was thinking. —Protect those who have come to help us, and guide us out of our despair— Lydee wondered whom the woman was addressing; Daiya's thoughts were little more than whispers. —Give us strength, and lead us to the right path—

Lydee raised her head and leaned on one elbow. Daiya was kneeling by the glowing embers, head bowed; she turned and saw the girl.

—I am praying— she explained.

Lydee was silent.

—Do not scorn me. I know that skydwellers look to the heavens and find no Spirit to watch over us. My faith is weak, but perhaps God will not judge me too harshly if I cling to what little I have. We may need even my prayers— She turned away, bowing her head once more.

The light stabbed her eyes; a shock stuffened her body. Lydee clawed at the air as she heard the screams. Her shield was weakening under the pressure of many minds. Reiho cried out; his arm struck her across the chest.

"What is it?" he called out.

Lydee rolled over him, stumbled up, and staggered toward the door, where Daiya stood silhouetted against the pale sky. Lydee struggled to restore her shield before the panic she felt swallowed her. A hand gripped her arm; Reiho was at her side.

"Something has happened," Daiya said. Her shield was so strongly buttressed that Lydee could not even mindspeak to her.

The three hurried outside. The sky beyond the black mountains was the colorless shade that preceded dawn; the village below seemed to be lighted by comets of flame as people ran through the streets with torches. At the edge of one field, several people were milling about near a watchfire, crying out with mind and voice.

At the center of the village, in the public space, ten giant robed figures stood, their heads towering over the nearest roofs; their arms were as long as the limbs of trees.

"Awake!" a voice trumpeted, and wind rustled the

grassy, thatched roofs. Lydee could hear the voice even at a distance, and sensed it inside of her as well. "You have slept too long. We waited for you to turn to Us, and instead you sought to forget Us. You sleep in fear, dreaming a nightmare that keeps you trapped between your old ways and the new possibilities open to you. Awake!" Other images flickered into existence near the huts and around the village; these were not giants, but several villagers were throwing themselves before the specters, hiding their faces in the dirt.

Reiho backed toward the hut. Another figure was taking shape in front of them, becoming a boy with long, black hair and pale, greenish eyes. Daiya cried out, covering her face.

—Daiya— the boy thought. —Don't you know me? I am Rin, your brother—

"I know you!" Daiya peered at him through her fingers. "You're dead. You died long ago in the desert, during your ordeal. You're an illusion."

—I am not. The Minds speak. You cursed Their silence, and now They answer you. The time of change approaches, and our people still sleep. Awake—

Another image was forming near Rin; the second specter was a boy in a silver suit. "No," Reiho whispered. Lydee stepped back on trembling legs and fell to the ground. Reiho was gazing at his former self, the Reiho who had died here.

"I'm going to die," Reiho said. "You've come to tell

me that I'm going to die again." The ghostly Reiho shook his head, holding out a hand.

"Rin!" Daiya cried. She reached toward the images, but they were already fading.

"Awake!" the giants below called out one last time before flickering out. The village was suddenly still. Then Lydee heard one long, low cry as over a thousand minds gave vent to their terror; the cry shattered, stabbing her with a million shards.

8

The villagers were crossing the meadow below the hill. A row of young people sat at the edge of the town, watching as the others moved past them. With each step, a few people would drop to the ground, sinking down in the grass, their heads blossoms among the green blades.

Lydee's head still hurt; the apparitions had upset her body's balance. She concentrated on the last vestiges of her pain, pushing them outside of herself. Reiho was staring fixedly at the villagers. Daiya's mind was silent.

Those leading the group had white, silver, or gray hair; their bodies were stooped, and a few were leaning on long sticks as they hobbled forward. More people sat down; Lydee recognized Silla and Harel. Marellon and Luret were sitting with a red-haired woman and a dark-haired man.

"They only want to see you," Daiya said. "The Minds have spoken, and my people must now try to reach out to you. You won't be harmed." Lydee wondered how the woman could know that; all of the villagers were concealing their thoughts.

Reiho was tense. Lydee could see his thoughts clearly enough; he was remembering death, recalling the time when the villagers had come for him. He looked back at the shuttle, which was still safely at the bottom of the hill, then turned toward the meadow. Most of the village was seated there now, waiting.

Only five people were climbing the hill toward them. "That is Cerwen," Daiya said, gesturing at the tall, broad-shouldered man in the front. "He's the oldest of the Merging Selves, and the rest of our people will see you through his eyes. He is also our grandfather."

The old man's gray hair was stiff and wiry; a gray beard hid the lower part of his dark-skinned face. Lydee's mental tendrils wound tight, becoming knots. Cerwen had ordered his granddaughter Daiya away from the village, had condemned her to a lonely life on this hill; what mercy would he show to another granddaughter who had become a skydweller? She sat still, legs folded, afraid to look directly at the man and apprehensive about meeting him in Reiho's presence.

Those with Cerwen also showed signs of age. One of the women had thick streaks of white in her dark-brown hair, while the man with her was round, with sagging jowls. The signs of age on Daiya had been disturbing enough; with a shock, she realized that none of these Earthpeople could be even as old as Etey.

The small group drew near. Cerwen surveyed Reiho briefly, then gazed more intently at Lydee. She was suddenly sure that he had grasped all of her thoughts in an instant. He sat down; the others sank down beside him.

—We are the Merging Selves— he said, and she knew that he did not mean only the four with him, but also many of those below on the grassy plain. The thoughts were not his alone, but all of theirs as well; Cerwen was only one aspect of the village, his individuality an illusion. She shivered. —I am Cerwen IviaRey, your grandfather, though I never thought to see you in this world, or even in the next— These words were not as forceful as his first statement.

—Greetings— she said, feeling how feeble her mind was next to his.

—These are other Merging Selves, whose thoughts I share. This woman is Leito SeyiNen— He waved at the slender woman with the white-streaked brown hair; her large eyes were as green as Luret's. Lydee sorted through what she knew of Luret's relations and saw that this woman had to be one of them. —And this

man is Morgen BianZeki— Cerwen gestured at the
pudgy man, who squinted at Lydee with his small,
dark eyes. —They, too, are your grandparents, for their
child is your mother. She is with us as well. She is
Anra LeitoMorgen, and her partner is your father and
my son, Brun RillaCerwen. It is strange for me to think
of them in separate guises, for we have drawn close—

She glanced at the younger couple, who sat a bit
apart from the others as though they had not merged
so completely with them. Anra LeitoMorgen was as
slender as her mother Leito, but her dark hair had only
a few strands of white and her pretty face was smooth.
Brun RillaCerwen was a short, stocky version of his
father. Lydee could see herself in him, the same brown
skin, the same brown eyes.

She fidgeted uneasily. Were they waiting for her to
show joy at the encounter? Anra and Brun were only
two people who had wanted her to die and had considered her birth an unfortunate event. Wrapping her
arms around herself, she tried not to think of how she
had been born.

Cerwen watched her calmly, seeming to be as patient
as a cometdweller with centuries of life in which to
speak. These people meant nothing to her; in spite of
their shared genes, they were only strangers, other villagers. To them, she was alien, a skydweller who needed
a link in order to share her mind with them.

—That is true— the five said in unison. —It is not

only blood that forms the ties of family, but also love and shared experience. Do not fear. We shall ask no more of you than we would of your companion—

—What do you want?— Lydee asked.

—We have spoken to manifestations of the dead— all of them answered through Cerwen.

—I saw my brother Dal— Anra said.

—I saw my mother Rilla— Brun said.

—I saw my friend Juhn— Morgen said.

—And I my father Nen— Leito murmured.

—Jowē spoke to me— Cerwen finished. —Jowē, who was the oldest of the Merging Selves before I became that, who fled this life when she beheld the skydwellers and heard the voices of Those under the mountains. And yet she was not Jowē as I knew her, for her mind no longer held the thoughts of the village and was no longer bound by our Net— He paused. —Skydwellers descend, the dead speak to us, and giants appear. What are we to do?—

—I don't know— Lydee answered, realizing that he was waiting for her suggestion.

—Then why are you here?—

—You know that she can't answer that— Daiya said. —She must wait with us to find out—

—I saw a vision too— Lydee said. —A woman told me that I must open myself to compassion and love— She frowned, knowing how hard that was going to be. She suddenly imagined Anra and Brun reaching out to crush her mind, destroying the solitary child they had not wanted. Even now, they scorned her; they had not wanted her to return.

—We do not scorn you, child— Cerwen said. —We are only confused about your purpose in being here—

—I think I am here to bridge the gap between your world and the comet—

Cerwen nodded; her other two grandparents, Leito and Morgen, were nodding with him. —We know that is what you believe. But how are you to do that? Clearly, it is possible for one here to be taken to the sky to live there and practice strange customs. It might also be possible for one to be brought here as a child, to grow up with no knowledge of that other world—

Lydee recoiled. She knew that no one on the Wanderer would consent to that, to bringing a child here to live, age, and die in such squalor.

—You see that there is still a barrier between us— Cerwen had read her thoughts. —We cannot break it down. It is you who scorn us—

—You wanted my death— Lydee replied. —No one on the comet would seek the death of another living thing. We don't even kill our animals. We have reason to scorn you, and I have more reasons than most—

Daiya gripped her with one mental strand, restraining her anger.

"Don't hold me back," Lydee continued aloud. "I can't hide my thoughts from you, so let me speak them. You would have preferred my death, and you wouldn't even allow Daiya to live among you. Did any of you protest that judgment?"

Cerwen's face was impassive. Leito's green eyes were glassy, while Morgen's reflected the look of an unthinking, instinctual creature.

"Did you protest it?" Lydee asked, turning from her grandparents toward Anra and Brun.

—You do not understand— Anra thought, while Brun pressed his lips together. —We must do what we think is right, however we may suffer—

—Lydee was a solitary— Daiya said. —Now she can mindspeak, and so can her companion Reiho. Other solitaries can be given that power, but only with the help of the skydwellers. That may be our bridge. Such people could live on Earth and yet have a bond with those above, and in time we might all grow closer. Solitaries do not have to die, and we don't have to bury them in the fields to be forgotten and condemned to eternal separateness—

Cerwen's mouth twisted. —We would welcome even the birth of a solitary now. At least that would show that we could still bear children. Your dream will die, Granddaughter, along with us, and the rest of Earth's people will erase our memory—

—You know why you have no more children—

Daiya said. —Your wills have failed you and turn your bodies against you. The future is dead in you. Rid yourselves of fear and despair, and the village will have its children—

—We would have them only if we could turn from what you have revealed to us and go back to the right way, but we are trapped in separateness and cut off from the rest of Earth. How can we bring more souls into the world only to condemn them to eternal separateness when it is time for them to leave their bodies?—

—The Minds have spoken to us— Daiya responded. —You have heard Them, too. We once believed God gave us our powers, but we have known for some time that it was our ancestors who actually gave us the power to use them. We cannot go back. We would live a lie—

Cerwen was silent. Anra, arms folded, gazed steadily at Lydee, who was suddenly aware that she was seated in exactly the same way. The five older people were pieces of her; she had Leito's hands, Brun's build, Morgen's round cheeks. If she looked deeply into their minds, she might find other resemblances, but they were all Merging Selves, and their minds had drawn so close to one another and to other villagers that she would not be able to tell which thoughts were their own.

She felt threatened by the group. She might have

forgiven them for having once wanted her dead, for they had not known any better, but she could not accept their similarity to herself. They would swallow her and force her to share their fate, which was that of the past.

A thread of compassion touched her; Brun's warm eyes were gazing in her direction. She refused to meet his glance. He had rejected two daughters, and Silla, the third, carried anger and hatred inside her. Brun and Anra might have taught Silla to care for Daiya, at least.

—I cannot go back to the comet— Lydee said at last. —I must share whatever awaits you. The Minds have imprisoned both Reiho and me, and will not let us go until whatever we are to do has been done—

—The Minds— She caught the bitterness in Cerwen's thoughts. —Why did They allow us to travel for so long on what we believed to be the right path, if it was wrong? Why did They then speak to us and bring evil days upon us, only to fall silent again when we needed Them most? And why do They come to us now in the guise of the dead and speak once more, only to leave the barrier around us?—

A strand of his mind touched Lydee, drawing her into his thoughts. She was conscious of the Net of thought that bound Cerwen and the other villagers; the Net's threads shook as they touched a cold surface. The old man was sensing the distant barrier, and could not reach beyond it.

—The wall is still there— Cerwen continued. —The Minds have not taken it away even now—

Abruptly, she withdrew herself from his mind and was inside herself again, wondering if she could have been trapped outside herself, unable to return.

—We shall not harm you, child— Cerwen said, responding to her thoughts. —We are at peace for now— Leito thought, adding to the chain of words. Morgen sent out a wave of wordless warmth, while Anra and Brun reflected the round man's sympathy, but their words and thoughts seemed distant from her, only the facets of one group mind. —We shall meet our punishment together— they finished.

—Let me say this— Daiya thought. —Once I traveled what I thought was an evil path, and I berated myself as you are doing now. If Reiho had not reached out to me and helped me, I would now be dead, and you might have lived out your lives without doubts. The Minds helped me when I needed Their help, and spoke to you—

Cerwen bowed his head.

—Reiho saved me from a death I sought for myself and restored me to you, and you repaid him by robbing him of his soul, which he still seeks. Now a daughter, a granddaughter has been given to you— Daiya held out a hand to Lydee. —That should be cause for some joy—

Anra reached for Brun's hand. Their eyes glistened, and for a moment Lydee knew that they were perceiving her as individuals without the intercession of Cerwen's thoughts.

—We can't go back— Daiya went on. —Our old lives were based on falseness and ignorance. We must prepare ourselves for new lives. If we must live them out behind the barrier, and those who follow us must do the same, then we'll do it, and eventually the wall will fall, even if it takes a thousand cycles, and we will have something new to show the world. We are being tested—

Cerwen stood up; his four companions rose with him almost in one movement. —We must pray— He turned toward Lydee, smiling a little; his eyes were gentle. —I see some traces of your human self, child, but also your solitude. You and your friend may come into the village whenever you wish. Visit our homes as guests, and touch our minds. Perhaps your only purpose, and that of your companion, is to dwell among us until you have become so like us that your skyworld is only a dream—

He turned and walked down the hill, the others trailing him. Knots of people were already making their way back to the village.

He can't be right, Lydee thought. She could not live here for years. If the shuttle failed for some reason and could not repair itself, she would have to depend entirely on Earth's food. Her body, strong as it was, would wear out eventually without treatment. She would age and die before her time. How could anyone accept that?

Reiho stared out at the meadow, then stood up and began to hurry down the hill toward the shuttle.

—We can't stay here— Lydee said. —Not for years—

Daiya shook back her long hair. —You had better accustom yourself to the idea. Did you think things would change right away? You know how long I have waited—

Lydee jumped up and ran after Reiho. The wild grass brushed against her legs as she passed. She recalled the groomed, orderly gardens of Home and longed for her cave. Homesmind had abandoned her; It had not even fought Earth's Mindcores for her. She screamed through her link, demanding her rescue. How could these people live like this? Even Daiya, who could have found a refuge on the comet, had chosen this world. The Earthfolk would never understand what Lydee had lost.

Reiho was inside the shuttle, staring at the panels. As she climbed inside, he slapped a hand against the ship.

"It won't take off," he said.

"You knew it wouldn't."

He looked up at her; his eyes revealed his rage. His anger shocked her; this place would unbalance them completely.

"Yes, I'm angry," he said, picking up her thoughts. "They've given up, haven't they? I wanted to strike out at all of them." He took a deep breath. "It's all right. I didn't want Daiya to see me this way—I was afraid I'd frighten her."

"She must have sensed how you felt."

"I suppose she did. I can't hide much from her. We'd better go back. She might worry."

She helped him out of the seat. As they climbed out of the shuttle, he took her arm. "I'm your mentor. I should have protected you instead of letting you come here. I might have come alone."

"It's better that we're together. We'll be braver that way, won't we?"

He gripped her elbow as they began to climb the hill.

9

—You must eat— Daiya said, waving a packet of food in front of Lydee. —And you've had no water—

—I can live without food for some time—

—You'll weaken yourself. You'll be of no use then. You have to maintain your strength—

Lydee accepted the package grudgingly and bit into a fruit bar. Daiya glanced toward the corner of the hut where Reiho lay on the mattress, his eyes closed. Rays shone through the openings under the roof; a band of light covered the man's chest.

—He is still in his trance— Daiya thought. Reiho had been lying in the corner for a night and most of the day.

—He's afraid to wake up— Lydee responded.

—He can dream of the comet and imagine this place is the dream—

—Poor Reiho. Even I can't tell whether it's this world he fears or his own reactions to it. But his former self was strong, and some of that strength is in him—

—You can awaken him, Daiya. I'm sure you know a way to penetrate his barrier—

—I'll let him be. I don't want to feel his pain when he opens his eyes and knows that he's still here, not yet. Sometimes a long sleep can heal the mind—

Lydee finished her food and stood up. —You're going into the village— Daiya continued.

—Cerwen told me I could. It's probably time I did—

—I see that you also want to go alone. Be careful, Lydee. There are many who still won't welcome you—

—I'm aware of that—

The sky was blue and unclouded; a warm breeze was blowing from the south. Several adults were in the fields, harvesting wheat. Tied bundles of grain lay on the ground as stooping figures, bending in unison, slashed with long curving blades.

In the center of the village, small groups had gathered to practice mindcrafts. A flower weaver was making wreaths for a few young people, binding the flowers with her mind, then dropping each wreath onto the head of a boy or girl. Others pointed as a dog passed them. It was walking on its hind legs and then bowing to them at its master's command. A few tables held bottles of wine; a few bottles floated toward outstretched hands as thirsty villagers passed.

Lydee descended the hill, suddenly aware of what the villagers had lost. Once, she supposed, they had done their tasks and played their games with joy, following their destined route through life, secure in their beliefs. The Merging Selves had taught and guided them; young people had looked forward to the time when they would live as their parents had. They had probably known peace as they aged, drawing closer to one another, believing that one day their souls would leave them to merge with the entity they called God or the Merged One.

Now their lives were only habit. They did what they had to do as if they were machines set into motion. They grew their food only because they had to eat, and seemed to take no pleasure in its cultivation. The gardens and vines near their houses grew fruit and vegetables, but few flowers. They clung to life because they were afraid to die, not knowing what judgment awaited them. Occasionally someone's mental shield would slip, showing Lydee the hollowness inside before the mind closed in on itself once more.

Daiya had given them knowledge of a world that traveled among the stars, and of the Mindcores that their ancestors had built and they had forgotten. They would have preferred certainty and ignorance.

She had sensed two familiar minds; one called to her. Lifting herself, she flew toward the riverbank at the edge of the village and landed near the water.

Luret glanced at her and smiled; Marellon nodded. They were naked; their freshly washed clothes hung suspended in the air, drying. The girl's skin was pink; Marellon was pale everywhere except for his light-brown hands, neck, and face. Several paces from them, two women were gathering water in buckets; their minds were closed, and they avoided looking at Lydee. Six old people sat under a tree, communing silently.

A dark-haired young man had come down to the river. Luret watched him as he filled his bucket; the corners of her mouth turned down. He gazed at her briefly before turning away.

—I've seen his face before— Lydee thought; his black eyes were familiar.

—You must have seen it in my mind— the Earthgirl said. —His name is Wiland IeuaGeve. Once we spoke of being partners, but we made no pledge— Lydee saw the rest before Luret closed her mind. She loved the young man, but Wiland had refused to commit himself to one whose mind held so much of Daiya's accursed wisdom. Luret still believed that Wiland loved her in spite of it. Lydee felt uncomfortable. These people seemed incapable of satisfying their physical needs without creating some elaborate emotional structure. Touching other minds, she thought, should have shown them how simple love was.

Marellon was staring at her. His face reddened and he turned away as if wanting to hide himself.

—Don't be shy— Lydee said. —We wear few garments on the comet and don't hide our bodies— His mind released the suspended clothes and they fell in a heap beside him.

—You wear a silver suit here— Luret said. She reached for Lydee's hand, pinching the skin. —And your skin isn't even real skin. You're completely covered. And you have added more clothes to all of that— She was laughing as she pulled at Lydee's sleeve.

—I wear these clothes only to look more like you—

—You hate your bodies so much that you've added things to them— Marellon picked up his tunic and pants and pulled them on, throwing Luret's clothes to her. —I thought that you might not care to look at mine—

—We don't hate our bodies. We only make them stronger and more durable—

—If you are so strong, why must you wear a silver covering?— His thoughts bore a challenge.

—It's only for protection— she replied. —I don't wear it on the Wanderer—

—Then why must you wear it here? Do you think anyone here can harm your body? I can sense your strength. And your mindpowers can guard you as well—

—I'm not invulnerable, Marellon—

—It isn't your body you have to guard, it's your mind. That's where you would be harmed—

Lydee frowned. —You're assuming that someone would try to harm me—

Marellon shrugged. —I've seen the thoughts of some. You think that your silver suit protects you, but it might only make you more careless. You should consider that, skydweller—

His argument made sense, she realized. She would have to learn to rely on this world's tools instead of her own.

She pulled off her tunic quickly, then took off her long pants. Turning toward the river, she opened her suit, peeling it from her skin until it lay in a shiny heap at her booted feet. Luret pointed at the boots and giggled. Lydee pulled on her clothes again, picked up the suit, folded the thin fabric, and thrust it into one of her deep pockets.

—You look more like us than I had thought— Marellon said. He was holding an image of her in his mind, but he was exaggerating some of her features, making her breasts rounder and her hips wider. Something else was at the edges of his thoughts; she sensed a wave of warmth before he put up his shield.

She sat down, trembling slightly. She would sweat and pick up dirt; she would wallow in this world, drawing closer to its minds and shedding the comet's civilization as she had shed her suit.

Luret's mind danced. —You made me think of a snake shedding its skin—

—Well, if I'm going to stay here, I'd better adapt as quickly as possible—

The two young people sat down near her. They smelled of reeds and the river; the odor was not unpleasant. She gazed at the river, studying its strong currents, thinking of the tamer river on the comet with its clear waters and tended shores.

—I feel sorry for you— Marellon thought.

She looked at him, surprised by his compassion.

—You are losing the world you knew— he went on, —and are trapped here, yet you aren't giving in to your fear. I feel you battling against it, but you hold it at bay. I try to think of myself trapped on your world, and I don't know if I could be as brave—

—I'm not brave. I'm trapped and trying to make the best of it— She gazed into his eyes, moved by his thoughts. His face seemed more attractive to her now; that realization suddenly embarrassed her. She lowered her eyes. —I was born here, after all. Maybe that makes it easier for me—

Luret turned her head, as if another mind had called to her. Harel KaniDekel was walking toward them. He stopped a few paces away and raised a hand, regarding Lydee with his blue eyes. —Greetings, Lydee AnraBrun, and welcome— He came nearer and sat down. Kindness and good will flowed from the man, but she also sensed a dark spot in his mind.

—Greetings— Lydee said.

His mind reached out to hers. —I see some of Dai-ya's spirit in you, and also some of her solitude— He was holding a memory of a young boy and a young girl sitting on a hill near the village, their minds bound in love. —She loved her solitude more than she loved me—

Lydee knew that wasn't true; Harel had rejected Daiya. His head jerked up. She had forgotten to shield her throughts properly, and they had turned into a blade, stabbing at the truth inside him. She cursed herself silently for her carelessness.

—She had become something different— the man said. —I would have bound her too tightly. I couldn't question things as she did. I couldn't live with her apart from the village. But I am still her friend— Harel had opened his mind almost completely, and she sensed his past self, the boy who had accepted the world without question, who had been undisturbed by doubts. The village's troubles had scarred him, leaving a dark abyss; without certainty and faith, he was lost.

Lydee, shaken by his thoughts, shielded herself. —You don't have to defend yourself to me—

—I have been punished for turning away from Daiya. I give my partner no children, and hide part of myself from her—I, who used to hide myself from no one. I can't show my love for Silla because she measures it

against what I felt for Daiya, but when I withdraw from
my partner, she berates me for my lack of feeling—

Their conversation had already revealed too much.
Lydee longed to cut it off, but was afraid of offend-
ing Harel. She had few enough well-wishers here.
—Couldn't you leave your partner then— she said
carefully, —and go to Daiya?—

Luret gasped. Marellon narrowed his eyes.

—I cannot— Harel murmured. —Silla is my partner. I still care for her. No one would willingly leave
a partner. If I can't love her fully, then I can't grow
to love others and will never be a Merging Self— The
customs of his world still bound him, even when he
lacked faith in them.

—That is a cruel custom— Lydee said.

—It is what we have always done—

—Why are you telling me this?— She knew almost
as much about this man as she had known about her
old friends, and perhaps more. She was learning to
reach out, as Earth's Minds had ordered. I have changed,
she thought, unable to imagine such an exchange with
any cometdweller.

—I am telling you this, Lydee, because you are like
Daiya—

His mind was clear and gentle; she saw why Daiya
had cared for him. Harel bowed his head; his mind
throbbed with pain. She wanted to ease him, but there
was nothing she could do.

Once again, she saw the image of Daiya as a girl forming in his mind; she and the young, beardless Harel were standing in the center of the village, bound to everyone else by strands of light. The villagers had shared their thoughts easily then, before Daiya's discoveries had brought them separateness.

—We are not the same— Harel said. —Even some of our Merging Selves too often fall into separateness now—

—I am sorry— Lydee thought. Taking a deep breath, she lowered all her barriers, reaching out to Harel, Marellon, and Luret, trying not to hold herself back. Through them, she sensed the strands that bound them to the village's Net, the web that tied them together even when they were lost in solitary musings. But another Mind was hovering over her, a Mind outside the Net; she tensed as It flowed into her.

—Be at peace— Lydee said, knowing that the thoughts were not her own. —You will pass through your ordeal and live again— As the Mind fled, her doubts returned.

Harel gazed at her with hope. —The Minds have spoken through you—

—Are you sure?—

—I am— He rose. —Come with me. It's time you saw more of our village—

They made their way along a dirt path between huts, passing vegetable gardens and then a fenced-in area where several pigs were feeding at a trough. A few passersby stared at Lydee silently as they passed; their minds were closed.

Some of the huts were longer and larger than others, big enough to house three or four families. The Merging Selves lived in those, moving from hut to hut as they wished, freer than others from family bonds.

Harel's hut was next to a chicken coop. Weeds grew along the short path leading to the doorway, and there were chinks in the hut's bricks. Lydee had noticed such signs of deterioration all along the dirt path, the outer signs of the village's despair; the smell of the latrines had nearly overpowered her. As they came to the hut's entrance, Silla hurried outside.

The wave of hostility flowing from the young woman was so strong that Lydee backed away, nearly tripping over a stone. Luret caught her arm, steadying her.

"You want to bring her inside," Silla shouted, still refusing to mindspeak to Lydee. The sound of her voice drew several neighbors to their doorways.

—She left her world to come here— Harel replied. —And she is your sister. We should try to welcome her—

"Not here. She's not welcome in our hut."

—Silla— Harel held out his arms. Already his mind had clouded as he concealed his inner thoughts from his partner. —She bears you no ill will. We have shared our thoughts, and the wall between her and Earth weakens—

"Listen to me." A few people had come outside and were now standing near their gardens, watching Silla. "I know why the skydweller and her companion were sent here, and it was not to share their unholy wisdom or to save us. Have they rid us of the wall that surrounds us? Have they brought us together? They have only divided us more. The Merging Selves dither among themselves, unable to act, and the rest of us wait. The Minds speak again, but don't tell us what to do. Well, I know what we must do now."

Lydee shook off Luret's hand and stepped back into the road, frightened by the wild look in Silla's brown eyes.

The Earthwoman raised her hand, pointing at Lydee. "We must take this skydweller and her friend to the field where we bury our dead and take their lives from them. Then all will see that we reject evil ways, and the wall will fall. That is why they were sent, to tempt us and test our souls."

—No— Harel thought. A few of the villagers had moved closer, apparently ready to carry out Silla's wishes immediately.

Lydee turned to run; invisible hands held her. Angrily she summoned her strength, preparing to strike, then hesitated. Her mind, drawing on her energies, could hurt many people before they overpowered her, and that would only enrage others. She threw up her wall, buttressing it as it shook under the assault.

—Stop— Harel thought, adding his power to Lydee's. —She shames you by not fighting back— Marellon and Luret were helping her to hold up her wall, but the claws of a beast seemed to scrape against it. —Will you strike at one who refuses to fight?—

"Leave her to me, Harel."

—No—

—Stop— That order came from a more powerful mind than Harel's. Silla's hands fluttered. The villagers backed away, looking uncertain and frightened.

Cerwen was walking down the path toward the hut. His dark face was composed, but his eyes were angry. —We have invited the girl to come among us, reserving our judgment, and you attack her. Are you going to make deceivers of us? You take too much upon yourself, Silla—

Lydee was still shielding herself, and could barely hear the old man's thoughts. She lowered her wall; the assault had been halted.

Silla glared at the old man, biting her lip. —You were wrong to tell her to come here, Cerwen—

—That is not for you to say, Granddaughter. The Minds have not ordered her death—

—The Minds haven't ordered anything. We are being tested—

—Leave her be— Cerwen's thoughts were weaker, as if he had withdrawn from the other Merging Selves.

"I can't fight you now," Silla said out loud, "but I

can wait. You'll see that I'm right." She glanced at Lydee threateningly, then went inside her hut.

—Go to your partner— Cerwen said to Harel. —Calm her thoughts if you can— Harel obeyed, following Silla inside.

Cerwen gazed at Lydee silently. —I am sorry for this— he said after a few moments. She could read his thoughts; sorry as he might be, he was also wondering if Silla might be right about her. The threat had not been removed, only deflected.

—She is not evil, Cerwen— Marellon thought. —You must see that—

—I see that she reaches out to us, and that her mind intends what she sees as good. But perhaps we have grown too separate to know evil when we see it— Cerwen turned and walked away, shielding his mind from them.

Lydee stared at her feet. —I had better go back to Daiya— The huts seemed to press in around her; she could feel those standing near her willing her to go.

—Stay— Luret said. —Come with us to our home. No one will strike at you now—

—I can't—

—You should— Marellon said. —You mustn't show fear now. They'll sense your weakness. You can't hide from them in Daiya's hut anyway—

She assented silently. Lifting her head, she faced the villagers standing behind the boy.

Marellon turned and gestured at one bony, older man. —Ede— he thought. —I've never known you to have violent notions— The man plucked at his shaggy beard. —And you, Karē— A blond woman hung her head. —You once asked the Merging Ones to draw Daiya back into our Net, and said it was cruel to leave her outside it. Are you going to hurt the one she's called here? And you, Areli— A stout woman folded her arms. —Maybe the evil is in you, not in this girl—

—You feared her yourself not long ago— the woman called Areli replied.

—We have exchanged our thoughts, and I no longer do— He broke off at that point. Taking Lydee's arm, he led her past the villagers as Luret followed.

This isn't the end of it, Lydee thought to herself. Outside her thin wall, she could sense the humming of the villagers' thoughts.

Nenla BariWil had just returned from the fields when the young people arrived at the hut; her partner Kal DeenēVasen was in the yard, scattering feed to the chickens. Their hut was at the edge of the village, bordering the fields; rosebushes grew at the sides of the dwelling.

Marellon greeted his sister. Nenla smiled at Lydee as she ushered her inside, seating her on a bench at a long, wooden table. Luret sat next to her mother while

Marellon began to set out food and drink.

—You are welcome here— Nenla thought, though her smile had already said that. Her long, red hair was pulled back from her freckled face; her kindly thoughts were a warm cloak over Lydee.

Kal entered the hut, shifting his broad shoulders as if fearful of finding the entrance too narrow. He glanced at his daughter. —I see that you have visited my cousin Silla— he said.

—Silla wouldn't let Lydee enter her home— Luret said.

Nenla nodded as she read her daughter's impressions of the confrontation. —It is not you she hates— she said to Lydee. —She looks within herself and fears what is there. She has one sister living apart from us, and now another who is a skydweller, and she thinks her own blood is cursed. She has no children because she believes that strain will reappear—

—But she wants children— Lydee replied, trying not to show how repellent that idea still was to her. —She said so when I first saw her—

—She thinks she does. But we have all been barren for a long time, each for a different reason. Some do not want to bring young ones into uncertainty, while others believe that they will bring forth only solitaries. I am Daiya's friend and know her doubts, and have come to accept the need for changing our ways, and yet it seems Luret will be my only child—

Kal touched Nenla's shoulder as he sat on the bench next to her, across from Lydee. —There will be time for more— he thought. Lydee stared at the tabletop, thinking that having even one child dragged out of one's body was quite bad enough.

She tried not to grimace as the family began to eat. Luret shoved a plate at her; Lydee shook her head. —Corn cakes— the girl thought. —I know you don't eat meat. And this is wine— She poured some into a cup.

Lydee sipped, not wanting to offend them, then nibbled at a cake. The red wine was robust and harsh; her teeth crunched against corn. Marellon was gulping his food, making sounds with his lips; he glanced at her as he was about to pick his teeth and put his hand in his lap. Luret gnawed at a chicken wing, cupping her hand as if trying to hide the repulsive sight.

—Silla is right about one thing— Lydee said. —I haven't been able to help you—

—The Minds have spoken to us again— Kal thought.

—Perhaps They would have spoken anyway. The wall still stands— Lydee paused. —When I was in the desert, I directed my mind at the wall, and it shifted. I might have torn a hole in it with help—

Nenla put down her cup. —Are you so strong?—

—With the aid of the whole village, we might be able to tear it down together. My strength would be added to yours, and that might be enough—

Kal shook his head. —Even if we could, we wouldn't be able to stand against all of Earth—

They finished the meal in silence. Lydee pushed her plate away, wondering if the food would make her sick; her stomach lurched. She fought the feeling with her mind, soothing herself. Kal and Nenla brushed against her with tendrils of thought; she felt their compassion.

—You aren't like the other villagers— she said.

—No, we are not— She sensed some bitterness in Kal's thoughts. His dark hair hung around his bearded face; he shook it back. —We too have fallen into separate ways. Some say we have listened to Daiya too much— He stood up and began to clear the cups and bowls from the table as Luret fetched the water bucket.

Lydee lay on a mat in the dark. In the hut's other room, Nenla and Kal were sleeping, their dreams entwined. Occasionally a strand of thought escaped from behind their mental wall, allowing her to glimpse their minds' embrace, a helix of jeweled bands.

Luret was asleep on a mat in one corner; Marellon was near the fireplace. Lydee stretched, trying to get comfortable. Her skin itched, and she dimly sensed the mechanical and instinctive minds of insects. She slapped at her arms and legs; now she would be infested, too.

Someone else was awake. She heard a rustling, then

felt warm breath near her ear. —You're still awake—
Marellon thought.

—I'm not used to sleeping on a mat, and my mind
is restless. I think of Silla and of all that Harel said.
Your emotions are strong here, and disturbing—

—I am drawn to you, Lydee— He took her hand.
—I don't understand it. It seems my feelings have
altered—

She put up her mental wall, leaving only a small
opening.

—I know that you don't see me in the same way,
and maybe you never can. You still see only a savage
with a weak body and unclean habits—

She drew her hand away. —Why are you telling
me this, Marellon?—

—Because you would have seen it in me anyway.
I am at the age when it's time to choose a partner, yet
I haven't found one. Others draw away from Luret and
from me because we seem unlike them. I thought that
I had grown too different from others ever to feel love,
and that my training with Daiya might have made me
too solitary. But you've shown me I was wrong. I can
feel love—

—You mustn't feel that way about me—

—And why not?— he asked.

—Because I can never be your partner. I can never
have children as your people do, and wouldn't even if
I could. I can't stay here, and if I did, you would grow

old while I remained young. Even without help from Homesmind and the comet, I would still live much longer than you—

—I ask nothing of you, Lydee. I only wanted to share my thoughts. It surprises me to feel this way about you—

—About one so strange— she said, picking up his uneasiness and embarrassment. His thoughts were turned in on themselves, as if he was trying to dim the glow shining at his center.

—Yes, you seemed strange at first. You seemed not to be human at all, and I saw you almost as a machine. Your mind was weaker then, and inside you an alien light glowed, as if another being lived there—

—Homesmind— she thought.

—But now I see your soul and know that it is like my own—

She suddenly wanted to reach out to him, but held back. Her strong feelings surprised her; she tried to tell herself that she was lonely and feeling only a momentary attraction. —You ask one person to cling to another until both are old and able to become Merging Selves—

—That's true— he replied.

—On the Wanderer, we are always free to love many—

—Yet you see into no one's mind—

—Yes—

—And you call that love?—

She thought of Pilo and Jerod, and her longing for her old life on the comet overwhelmed her. What would those boys, and Nara and Tila, think if they could see her now, lying on a mat in dirty clothes with Earth's food in her belly, huddling near an Earthboy and able to feel some love for such a creature?

Marellon's wall went up. —Do you think I would choose to feel this way about you, skydweller? I'm sorry I shared my thoughts with you. Don't worry. I won't inflict them on you again— His mind throbbed; she had wounded him.

—I'm sorry— she thought, knowing that would not make up for the hurt. He retreated to his own mat while she curled up and tried to sleep.

A clap of thunder awoke her. Lydee sat up, blinking. Light flashed through the hut's openings and illuminated the doorway.

Someone screamed. Feet padded across the floor; as the lightning flashed again, she saw Kal's broad form in the doorway.

She stood up and stumbled toward the entrance. People were running through the street toward the center of the village. Another cry pierced the air. She kept her mind closed, afraid to let the village's panic flow into her. Kal hurried outside, followed by Nenla.

Marellon was near her. "What's going on?" she said aloud.

—I don't know— She could barely hear his thoughts.

—The Merging Selves are calling to us—

Lydee stumbled outside. Several people were running through the fields toward her while the watchfires they had been tending flickered in the distance. Rain came swiftly, pouring from the sky in cold, sharp needles; the wind shrieked. Lightning forked across the heavens.

Slowly, she let down part of her shield. A thousand minds babbled, —The wall! The wall!— Through the villagers' Net, she now sensed the force field and understood why they were afraid. The wall was inside the mountain range, a day's travel closer to them on all sides. A few minds were already struggling to push it back.

She fell against one villager and was suddenly swept forward by the crowd. She closed her mind quickly. "Marellon!" she screamed, trying to free herself from the press of bodies. Losing her balance, she tripped and fell forward, clawing at the mud as feet trod on her back. She rolled toward a hut and staggered up, uninjured.

Marellon was running to her, Luret close behind him. Wind buffeted her, pushing her against the boy; the path was littered with thatching. They followed the stream of people, slipping in the mud as the rain drenched them.

The village's public space was lighted. Several people stood in doorways or under booths, shielding their torches from the rain. Several Merging Selves, Cerwen among them, stood on tables in the center of the mob, their faces tense with effort as they pushed against the barrier.

"It's gone!" a man cried triumphantly. Lydee clutched at the Net with her mind and abruptly sensed the barrier again; it was now on the other side of the river and closing in around the fields; the village would be crushed inside it. "No!" the same man screamed.

"Steady your mind!" a woman shouted.

Lydee added her strength to the villagers', realizing how futile their effort was. The force field was now a wall around the edge of the town, cutting them off from the river and the fields.

She pushed. The field had stopped moving, though she was sure their feeble efforts had not halted its progress. Several Merging Selves had collapsed; others lifted them from the tables and laid them on the ground, trying to revive them. They were completely enclosed inside the village.

—We are locked here— Cerwen thought. Marellon trembled; Luret sagged against him. Lydee stood with them at the edge of the crowd, sensing their shock.

Gradually she became aware of another mind boring through the little of her shield she had left. She turned. Most of the crowd was kneeling, clinging to one another for solace. Silla was standing, her shadowed eyes gazing directly at Lydee, her face yellowish-brown in the light.

"You brought this on us, skydweller." Silla raised one arm and pointed. "You came into our village, and now the wall traps us here. I was right. You must die before we are freed." Others stood up and moved closer to Silla.

—You are a fool— Marellon thought rashly. —The wall surrounded us before Lydee arrived. It could not have been her doing—

Lydee held her hands out, pleading silently with Cerwen. He was wavering, looking from her to his other granddaughter.

"Cerwen!" Lydee cried. "Let me add my strength to yours, and try to break this wall." She did not trust herself to mindspeak, afraid that her thoughts would free themselves from her and lash out at Silla.

"We can't break the wall," Silla responded. "We have tried."

"Don't you understand? We must break it somehow." She looked at Cerwen. "Daiya and Reiho are outside the wall now. If we don't get to them, every mind outside the wall will be able to direct its force against them."

10

Silla lifted one hand to her mouth, then turned toward Cerwen. —They are doomed— he said. —We cannot reach them—

"Maybe we can," Lydee replied. "If I add my strength to yours, that might give us just enough power to break through. At least we can try."

—How can we draw on the power we need?— one mind demanded; she recognized Brun. —Hasn't the wall now cut us off from the mountains, the source of our power?—

Lydee frowned. "We cannot be cut off," she said. "If we were, you would not be able to mindspeak at all." Earth's Minds were still helping them somehow. A more disturbing thought came to her; if the Mindcores could still reach them, then why hadn't They broken the barrier? Why were They allowing the village to be subjected to this new threat?

Cerwen nodded, reading her thoughts. —We are asking ourselves these questions— he said. —Perhaps They have the power to open another channel to us, but cannot break the wall Themselves. I don't know. They seem willing to let us suffer—

"I can answer your questions, skydweller," Silla said; she had apparently touched Lydee's mind even though she was still refusing to mindspeak. "We have been left our powers so that we may kill you more easily."

—Please— Lydee called out with her mind. —We must try to break the wall and find Daiya and Reiho—

"And bring another cursed skydweller here? Let him die."

—Daiya's out there, too—

—What's Daiya to us?— one burly man was thinking. —She is not part of the Net, and has lived outside the settlement communing with herself. Let her reap the harvest of her solitary ways—

—She's your sister— Lydee said to Silla. —Do you care so little for her?—

"She's probably dead," Silla replied, but Lydee could tell that the young woman was uncertain. She directed her thoughts at the mire of guilt inside Silla; her jealousy had nearly swallowed her love for her sister, but there was still a little love left.

The rain fell more slowly, becoming a drizzle. The

sky was growing lighter; a mist blurred the figures around Lydee.

Harel rose; beads of moisture gleamed on his beard and hair. —I'll help you— he said. —I'll try as hard as I can to help you break through the wall— He turned toward Silla. —And so will you. If you don't I'll leave our home and never touch your mind again—

Several people gasped at Harel's threatened breach of custom. Silla held out a hand; her mind was raging, twisting in pain as her need for her partner contended with her fear of the skydweller.

—We must try to open the wall— Lydee said. —All of us, for every mind will be needed, and all of your wills. If we can tear a hole in it, I'll go outside and search for my mentor and my sister. If your God and your Mindcores will it, then I'll die out there, and you, Silla, will have your wish—

Silla lowered her eyes.

—Draw together— Cerwen thought. —Direct your minds at the wall. Lydee, you must go to the edge of the village, and we shall lend you our strength—

Brun and Anra were making their way through the crowd, elbowing those who were standing and stepping over the ones who were seated. —We'll come with you— Brun said.

—You mustn't— Lydee protested.

—You may need our help to shield you from harm— Anra murmured.

Brun waved a hand. —Our daughter is out there.

She turned from us and brought us evil days, but she is still our child. We gave her life and will share her fate—

—I'll go, too— Marellon thought.

—And I— Luret said. Kal cried out a protest; Nenla shook her head.

—No, Luret— Marellon said. —I am older and have a little more practice in mindcraft. If anything happens to me, at least my sister will have her child—

Luret shook her head. —If you don't come back, we'll all die behind this wall anyway— Her mother's arms were already around her, holding her back.

—Go— Cerwen commanded. —Don't waste your power in bickering. We must act now. If Daiya is still in this world, she will be draining herself of energy trying to stay alive—

Lydee ran along the muddy path toward the meadow, Marellon beside her. Anra and Brun were behind them, somehow managing to keep pace in spite of their age. Sparks danced in the air around them as the villagers gathered their strength.

They might be taking this risk for nothing; Daiya and Reiho might already be dead. Lydee suppressed her doubts, which would only blunt her ability to strike at the wall. She did not even know if a hole could be torn in the field; she tried not to think of that, either. She had to believe it was possible and remembered what she had been able to do to the wall alone in the desert.

They came to the edge of the village; her knee struck the invisible barrier. A fog hung over the meadow outside; Daiya's hill was hidden behind nature's misty wall. Lydee scowled; she had been hoping that they would find Daiya and Reiho near the force field, trying to find a way inside.

A hand gripped her shoulder; she glanced at Brun. Anra, the tallest among them, stood straight, staring at the wall as if she could pierce it with her eyes.

Lydee opened her mind, bracing herself against the wall with both hands. The villagers drew her into the Net; its bonds were heavy cables tying her to each mind. She pushed at the barrier, letting the power flow through her, trembling as she felt its force.

A spot began to glow around her hands. Heat seared her palms; she pulled her hands away, visualizing the atomic structures that held the field together. The wall was weakening; she summoned more power, directing it into the Net. Her link burned and her bones ached with the effort. The glowing spot grew larger.

She was at her limit and knew she had only enough strength left for one last push. Straining, she forced her mind at the wall, making a knife of her thoughts.

The wall ripped; wind slapped her face. She fell through the opening and rolled across the grass, striking a lump of dirt. The others followed, stumbling over her as she lay on the ground. She had exhausted herself; she could not move.

She threw up her mental shield quickly, sensing that her companions were doing the same. Marellon was beside her, lying on his back. She lifted her head. Anra and Brun lay face down; she was suddenly afraid the effort had been too much for them.

At last Brun moved, propping himself up on one elbow. She probed for his thoughts; he shook his head. "No, child. Don't use your mind to speak. We must shield ourselves thoroughly so that no one knows we are outside." She felt as though something was poised over her and imagined a hammer about to pound her into the ground. Quickly, she thrust the image from her, afraid her own thoughts would turn against her.

Marellon stirred; his strength was returning. She fed him some of her power, then lent more to Anra. The older people were badly weakened; Brun's shield seemed thin.

"The wall has mended itself," Brun whispered. He and Anra were cut off from the other Merging Selves and the Net. They would need some of her power, and she had little to give.

They were still alive, at least. Either the Earthfolk on this side of the wall had not yet sensed their presence or they were waiting until those who had broken through grew too tired to resist. They would have sensed a rip in their wall, she was sure, but might be too far away to notice four small, shielded minds. Lydee began to hope.

She stood up. Their shields were stronger now; if they could keep them up, no one would be able to sense their presence. Now they would have to get to the hill; they could not even search with mental strands to find out if Reiho and Daiya were still alive.

Reaching out, she helped Anra to her feet. The woman held on to her tightly and seemed about to speak, but did not. Brun leaned against Marellon.

"Are you ready?" Lydee asked. Brun nodded. "Then we must go."

The four locked hands as they moved toward the hill. The mist surrounded them, blotting out the world. Lydee longed for sensors, afraid they might lose their way. The wet grass brushed against her trousers; her soggy clothes clung to her body.

They have to be alive, Lydee thought as her legs churned through green weeds. Reiho might have given in to his fears when he realized what was happening. Even Daiya might not have been able to save him. She walked more quickly, tugging at the hands in hers, feeling the rough calluses on both Marellon's and Brun's palms. Marellon shivered; the hands holding hers were cold. They could not even free their minds to warm the air; she wondered how the older couple would fare in the dampness.

"You are good to help us," Brun said. "I had thought that you were only trying to run from Silla's wrath, but when I touched your mind, I saw that it wasn't so. There is caring inside you."

She squinted. The mist was lifting a little; she could now make out the hill. She pulled at the others, wanting to run forward.

"Save your strength," Anra said. "We must still climb the hill."

Lydee slowed. There was still no sign of her sister or her mentor. They struggled toward the slope.

Brun was panting. Lydee had one arm around his waist, urging him on. The mist was a thin veil; the trees around Daiya's hut were robed in gray.

Lydee let go of Brun, crying out in dismay. A tree had fallen across the roof of the hut; one of the walls had caved in. She ran to the doorway ahead of the others and peered into the darkness, afraid of what she might find.

"Reiho?" she called out. "Daiya?"

A moan answered her. She rushed inside, nearly stumbling over a mound of bricks. A light suddenly shone in her face; she threw up an arm.

"Lydee," Reiho's voice said. The light darted across the caved-in roof and came to rest near a pile of rubble. Reiho was holding a light wand. A beam of wood lay across his chest, pinning him to the ground; if he had been an Earthman, he would have been crushed by it. Daiya was next to him, her leg trapped under the same beam; her eyes were closed.

"You're alive," Lydee said. "And Daiya—"

"She's alive, too. But we're weak. We've both been shielding our thoughts all this time—Daiya said that was what we had to do. I see we're all trapped outside the force field now."

"We were inside it. We broke through the wall, just for an instant, just long enough to get through to you." Her companions were in the doorway; she motioned to them. "Help me move this beam."

"I tried to move it," Reiho said. "I couldn't get leverage. Be careful, or you might bring more bricks down. Just lift it a little—I can crawl out."

Brun and Marellon braced themselves against the beam as Anra leaned over Daiya. Lydee knelt, pushing against the wood. The beam lifted with a slight creak and Reiho wriggled out from under it while Anra freed her daughter. Lydee lowered the beam slowly as dirt and thatching sprinkled them.

Daiya's eyelids fluttered. "She's hurt," Reiho said. "She's been using all her strength to shield herself. I didn't know what was happening at first." His voice tripped over the words. "Somehow I managed to push Daiya out of the way before—"

"Don't waste yourself in talk," Anra murmured. "We must get back to the village. Can you walk?"

Reiho nodded. "But I don't think Daiya can." He dropped to Daiya's side, feeling her leg. "Her leg's broken."

"The shuttle." Lydee ran to the door and hurried outside. The mist was fading; strands of gray gossamer were settling on the green ground. As she made her way down the slope, she peered toward the spot where the shuttle should have been. The craft could carry them to the village; she would have to hope that their enemies could not sense it if they kept a shield around themselves. She might be able to move it with her mind if the others protected her with their walls.

Where was the ship? She looked around frantically, darting to another side of the hill, then spied the shuttle's dome. She nearly dropped her wall when she saw what had happened. The shuttle had somehow been swept toward Daiya's garden and was tilted on one side, its runners embedded in a vegetable patch. They would have to strain to move it. She pressed a fist against her mouth.

"Lydee!" She looked up. Marellon had come outside and was standing on the hill above her. "Daiya's failing—she can't keep her shield up much longer. We have to go now."

"The shuttle." She waved her arms helplessly.

"Forget your vessel. We need all our power to help shield Daiya."

She climbed toward him as Brun carried Daiya outside. Lydee motioned to him. "Reiho and I can carry her." She went to her sister. Daiya sagged against her as Lydee gripped her waist, then helped Reiho lift the woman's legs.

"Link minds," Brun ordered. "We have to weave ourselves together now, and shield Daiya as well. If they track her mind, we are lost."

Together, the group struggled down the hill.

Their minds were wedded. Lydee touched Brun's stoic thoughts, sensing his grim determination; his mind was now part of her own, locked there by the links they had formed. Daiya had brought him grief, but he would not leave his daughter to die alone. Anra's thoughts were simpler; she would do what she could, and the rest was in God's hands. Marellon was thinking of the village, willing himself to keep up his strength long enough to get there, refusing to doubt that he would; he would prove himself to Lydee. Reiho's energy was being drained by his fear of death as he worked to maintain their mental wall.

Daiya was barely conscious as they came to the meadow and began to cross it. Her head drooped; her long, matted hair hid her face. The arm around Lydee was flaccid, unable to grip.

The sky was lighter; the fog had nearly burned off, and Lydee began to feel conspicuous, imagining thousands of invisible observers. She buttressed her shield as she bowed her head, concentrating on her feet, thinking only of the next step she would take and then the one after that. The village seemed far away, the pressure against their shield greater. She began to count her steps, giving up when she came to thirty.

Anra patted her arm, but her eyes were on Daiya. Anra still saw the woman as a child. We'll get you home, she was thinking, and her thoughts entwined with Lydee's; we'll get you home safely. Anra's thoughts blurred at that point, becoming a series of vague images in which she, Brun, Daiya, and a young Silla sat in a hut, minds bound together again, differences forgotten. Another figure lingered at the edges of this picture, a person of wire and glass with dark eyes, and Lydee realized that was how Anra saw her.

"I understand now," Anra whispered. "You are our daughter, too."

Lydee did not reply.

"Don't waste your strength in talk," Brun muttered.

They were closer to the village. Cerwen and Harel were waiting just inside the force field, with other villagers gathered behind them along the path. Leito and Morgen rushed to Cerwen's side.

Daiya's mind suddenly dropped out of their web; she had fainted. Lydee drew on more energy, strengthening their wall.

Cerwen signaled, pointing at the force field, then at them. Brun motioned to his father, and Lydee understood what the signals meant. They would have to direct their thoughts at the wall at the same time the villagers were boring from within, and that meant they would have to drop their mental shield. They would be open to attack, uncamouflaged. If the field did not fall, they would die. She hoped that they had the strength to break through.

"Don't think of that, child," Brun said. "We'll need all of your power. We broke through before and can do so again."

Lydee nodded, wanting to believe him. They stumbled up to the wall and lowered Daiya's legs to the ground, still holding her by the waist. A wind was rising on the meadow; the grass rippled.

Cerwen raised his arms; Brun pointed at the invisible barrier. —Now— he thought.

Their mental shields dropped as they aimed their thoughts. Lydee pushed at the wall. The wind screamed around her as claws tore at her mind. She drew more strength; the wind howled a protest. Marellon fell to the ground, writhing; the barrier began to glow. Pain shot through her as the wall was torn; the sound of the ripping nearly deafened her.

Cerwen's arms reached out to Marellon. Anra pulled the boy up and thrust him at the old man, then pushed Reiho toward Harel. Lydee screamed, dropping Daiya as she doubled over in pain, pressing her hands against her head, afraid that her skull would explode. Brun picked up his unconscious daughter and handed her to the villagers.

Lydee was failing. Her strength was gone. The hole began to close, the fire at its edges burning more fiercely.

Anra yanked her arm; Brun grabbed her shoulders and aimed her at the flames. She cried out as the fire seared her; hands slapped at her burning hair as minds quenched the fire. Someone pulled her up; she gazed into Nenla's face. She was inside the shield.

She sat up. The force field had closed. Anra and Brun were still outside, eyes pleading as their fists struck the wall.

"We have to open it again," Lydee said desperately. Several people had already collapsed from the effort; Leito was kneeling beside Morgen, weeping as she rubbed his chubby wrists. Lydee could sense the weakness in the Net. She forced her thoughts at the wall, knowing she had hardly any strength left.

Anra turned to Brun. He lifted her hands to his face, then drew her to him. Their lips moved; they were smiling.

"No," Lydee wailed, realizing that the two were preparing for death.

The wind outside gusted soundlessly. A funnel of dark clouds danced across the meadow toward the couple. Lydee's muscles locked; her mind shattered. A piece of her, its strength gone, watched as the whirlwind swept up Anra and Brun and then fled, becoming a stream of gray mist mottled with the redness of blood.

11

Lydee sat outside Nenla and Kal's hut, gazing at the field outside the invisible wall. Stalks of corn had begun to ripen; a few stray cattle and sheep were already grazing near the crops. Feebly, she probed the force field with her mind before withdrawing behind her mental shield.

Reiho emerged from the hut. She had not sensed his movements; she kept her shield up constantly, unable to bear the pain that throbbed in the minds around her. Kal's father Vasen, brother to Anra, had come to the hut that morning to see Daiya; he had left quickly when he had seen Lydee and Reiho there, and she wondered if he was blaming them for Anra's death. Daiya had muttered all night in her dreams as Nenla and Kal tried to help her heal.

Reiho sat down next to her, hugging his legs. "Daiya still won't speak to me," he said in their own language. Daiya had been sitting in one corner, refusing to speak, shaking her head as if communing with someone no one else could see. Lydee had been unable to break through her sister's wall. Even Nenla and Kal had finally retreated for the day, taking Marellon and Luret with them to the public space.

"We should have brought the food we left in Daiya's hut," Lydee said. "I should have gone down to the shuttle and taken out more supplies. We might have tried to get it here somehow."

"We wouldn't have made it."

They were cut off from the shuttle, their lifeline; she wondered if the Earthfolk outside had already torn it apart with their minds. The rest of Earth might be showing them mercy by allowing them the chance to take their own lives, or they might simply be gathering their resources for a final assault. Maybe they had weakened themselves in moving their wall closer to the village and were now waiting to grow strong again.

"We may die," Reiho went on. "Just like those others." She bowed her head. A few of the villagers were dead along with Anra and Brun, and some of the gardens bordering the public space were now graves for the five Merging Selves and the two younger people whose efforts to tear at the force field had robbed them of their lives. Morgen BianZeki had been among the victims. Lydee had watched as the village had gathered to mourn. Leito and Cerwen had wept together for him and for their children Anra and Brun.

"The people here think that they will join their God and live on in another life," Reiho murmured, "but we know that isn't true. All that awaits us is nothingness." He glanced at her. "It may be easier for Earthfolk to be brave. They have more to look forward to and less to give up."

Lydee took his hand. "You helped us save Daiya. She wouldn't even be alive now without your help."

"I wish I could have done more." He sighed.

"The Mindcores will help us—They can't leave us like this." But even as she spoke, she was thinking of Anra and Brun. They had reached out to their daughter Daiya at last, only to be snatched away at the moment of reconciliation. Her throat tightened. Toward the end, Anra had even reached out to Lydee, attempting to make amends to the child she had once wished dead; the couple had saved her life by pushing her through the closing gap in the force field. She swallowed hard. The Mindcores had not even tried to save them. Morgen, her other grandfather, was dead, and she had not had a chance to know him.

She recalled the faces of the two who had been her parents. Even the cometdwellers might have found Anra's fine features pleasing if they could have overlooked the signs of age, the tiny lines etched lightly around her eyes. Brun's gentle, dark eyes had looked out of a bearded face seemingly struggling to be stern. They had smiled as the whirlwind swallowed them; they had shown no fear. Their minds, no doubt, had already been looking beyond this world, clinging to their superstitious beliefs. They had only deceived themselves. Had they known that this life was all they had, they might have made it through the wall. They might have fought harder to live.

"I know what we have to do," she said wildly. "We must break through the wall again and go outside, then offer ourselves to this village's enemies. We can ask them to spare the village in exchange for our lives and tell them that the people here will turn from their doubts."

Reiho shook his head. "We can't tear the wall open. The people here are too weak now, and cannot summon the strength. And do you think those outside would spare the village? They killed Anra and Brun, who clung to old ways as much as anyone here could from what Daiya has told me. And the village can't just forget its questions. They can't hide their doubts and still allow others to touch their minds." He paused. "Do you really think you could go outside and meet death so willingly?"

"No." Her impulse was fading. She did not want death, only an escape. Even now, she could not imagine herself swallowed by oblivion; perhaps no one could until the moment was upon her.

"We shall not die," a voice said in the Earth tongue.

Lydee turned. Daiya was standing in the doorway, leaning on a long, wooden pole. Her face was drawn and sallow; her eyes stared past them at the field.

"We shall not die," Daiya said again, sounding unlike herself; her voice was low, but strong. "I hear the dead, and know that they live. The Merged One will not abandon us, and the Minds under the mountains are still linked to us. I have seen Anra and Brun, and they have told me not to mourn."

"They're dead," Lydee burst out. "You couldn't have seen them."

"Yes, I know. Nenla showed me how they died. I tried to push her mind from me, but she forced me to see. Now I know that they loved me after all. When death came for them, they were reconciled with me and yet had not lost their faith—they were as close to a holy state as one can be in this life. They died together, as they would have wished, and they are still together, two thoughts in the mind of God."

"You say that," Lydee responded. "You, who doubt."

"Yes, I have doubts." Daiya's voice was softer now. "When I meet my death, maybe there won't be another life for me, but those who are like my mother and father may live on. In this life, we create the fate of our souls—our minds shape it. I'm healing now. I won't give in to despair again. It always passes, you see. We'll live."

Daiya had been driven mad. That was all Lydee could think as she looked at the woman's face. Daiya seemed transfixed, her eyes gleaming with a barely restrained hysteria. Frightened, Lydee shrank against the hut; anything she would say might only provoke her sister.

"I must go to the Merging Selves," Daiya continued in a toneless voice. "We must prepare ourselves and wait for a sign." She limped toward the road, leaning on her stick.

"But you're hurt," Lydee protested. "You must—"

"Let her go." Reiho's hand came down on her arm. In their own language, he said, "Let her believe what she must. It doesn't matter now. I only wish we could cling to such a delusion."

Lydee stood on a line with Marellon and Luret, waiting as those in front of her inched forward. The villagers near them were sullen and passive. The young man called Wiland shot Lydee a harsh glance, then turned away, ignoring the hand Luret had raised in greeting.

Three days had passed, and the sign Daiya was expecting had not appeared. Lydee could scarcely bear to be near her sister now. Daiya continued to mutter to herself at intervals, and it was impossible to tell if she was praying or cursing. The villagers were still stunned by their predicament, passively obeying the Merging Selves; Lydee wondered how many others would soon go mad.

Cerwen and the other Merging Selves had assembled the village's remaining provisions in the public space, pouring water into barrels and piling food onto tables. Cerwen had put aside his personal sorrow in order to reassure everyone, noting, as the lines were forming, that there was a large quantity of new wine, that several villagers had saved water from the storm, that wheat had recently been harvested, and that there were many chickens, ducks, and pigs inside the barrier. If they gathered what was in their gardens and rationed their supplies, they could survive for some time.

She tried not to think of what would happen when the day came, as it eventually would, when all the supplies were exhausted. The water might be the first thing to go; they were cut off from both the river and the field's ditches. They would have to hope for more rain, even though the force field was likely to prevent much of it from reaching them.

Lydee fidgeted, plucking at her hair; the singed ends were dry and brittle. She was enclosed in this village; the stink of the bodies around her was almost more than she could bear. She looked down at her dirt-stained tunic; she was as filthy as the rest.

What were the Earthpeople outside waiting for? If they had enough strength to enclose them inside the force field, they could, with only a little more exertion, crush them entirely. That thought made her shudder. Luret glanced at her, concern in her green eyes. The wall already seemed closer.

They moved forward and found themselves in front of Leito. Luret greeted her great-grandmother while Marellon handed the old woman their waterskins. Leito filled them, then took the skin they had given to Lydee.

"Now we give skydwellers our precious water," Wiland said.

—Silence yourself— Leito's green eyes narrowed. —They are trapped here with us and will share what we have— Wiland scowled as he accepted provisions from another old woman, then hurried away.

—Two days— Leito thought, handing Lydee her water and directing them to Cerwen, who was helping to hand out food. —Your water must last you that long— Lydee frowned, already feeling thirsty. She would not have much to drink; bathing would be impossible.

Luret and Marellon accepted a roasted chicken from Cerwen; Lydee averted her eyes from the dead, plucked fowl. The old man held out a small pouch of corn; she shook her head, refusing it.

—It's little enough for two days— Cerwen thought.

—I can go without food for a while—

Cerwen did not insist, turning to the next villager as the three young people walked out of the public space. Reiho was saving one last small packet of food out of the two he had found in his pockets and had promised to share it with her later. After that, she would be forced to eat village food, and when the grain and fruit gave out, she might be reduced to eating meat. The thought nauseated her. She wondered exactly how long she could go without food before her body began to weaken; Homesmind could have told her.

—The skydwellers have brought us death again— The thought was sharp. She looked back at the line of villagers, trying to see who had thought it. —When they came, we should have sent them away and punished Daiya for bringing them—

—Don't heed such notions— Marellon said to her.

—They may be true—

—Don't think that—

She stopped near one garden and turned to him. —I'm helpless now. Without the shuttle, I'm more helpless than you—

—I think— Luret replied, —that we are all equally helpless—

Lydee awoke, feeling uneasy. The air was still, as if a storm were about to break; her neck prickled. Reiho stirred next to her; Marellon and Luret were sitting up. Daiya still slept.

—Do you sense it too?— Luret asked.

Lydee nodded. Someone was outside, waiting, but the thoughts of that person were shielded. She got up and went to the doorway, feeling as though she was being drawn there against her will.

A small crowd had gathered outside the hut, Silla at its head. Wiland was with her, along with a tall, pale woman from one of the neighboring huts, two older people, and several young men and women. Reiho moved closer to the doorway and peered out at the villagers.

"What do you want?" Lydee said aloud, trying to keep her voice calm.

"Come outside," Silla replied.

Lydee walked toward the crowd, stopping a few paces away. Silla's eyes narrowed. "What is it you want?" Reiho called out.

"We've come for you, skydwellers. It is time."

Lydee threw up a wall around her mind. "Time for what?" she said faintly, though she already knew.

"Time for you to meet your deaths," Silla said.

Reiho made a sound of protest. Lydee glanced back at him as he sagged against the doorway. Luret suddenly pushed past him, followed by Marellon. —Leave them alone— the girl thought.

"Do you want to fight us, too?" Silla asked. "It's time to rid ourselves of this curse. If you fight us, we'll take your lives as well."

"You aren't strong enough," Marellon said.

"Stay out of this," Wiland said, and then more softly, "I don't want to hurt you." He was looking at Luret, who gazed back with angry eyes.

"Do you think you can frighten us away?" Silla shouted. "We are already dying. Our food and water will run out, and then we'll starve and spend our last days in a prolonged agony. If we die assaulting these skydwellers, we will either be reunited with God for having done the right thing or we'll lift this curse." She folded her arms. "For the first time in my life, I am glad I have no children to witness such evil days."

"The evil is in you, sister." Daiya was at the doorway, leaning on her stick. Lydee watched her, surprised; Daiya's eyes were clear and her voice had its old resonance. "Go away, Silla. You don't know what you're doing. We mustn't fight now, but should draw closer."

"How can you say that? Have you forgotten Anra and Brun so quickly? They died because of that girl and that man."

"I live because of that girl and that man. And Anra and Brun helped her willingly. The Minds under the mountains will not ignore our need—you must believe me."

"I have touched your thoughts," Silla replied. "You are mad, Daiya, and your mind creates false images and false hopes. I think you are hoping for my death so that you can go to Harel. I see that we must fight you, too."

Reiho was pale. Lydee sensed his agitation; he was

already seeing the death he had expected. Kal suddenly appeared behind him as Nenla came outside.

"Go, Silla," the red-haired woman said firmly. "These skydwellers are guests in our home. I can't let you harm them."

"You don't frighten me, Nenla. You and my cousin Kal have grown separate from us for a long time. You'll only die with them."

Lydee's hands were fists; she kept them at her sides, longing to strike out at Silla. Many people could die in a battle; others might join in. A few were already gathering outside the nearest huts, waiting to see what would happen; if the villagers lashed out at one another during the fray, even the Merging Selves might be unable to stop it.

"I won't fight you," Lydee said, feeling as if the words were being torn from her. "If you've come for me, then try to take me. But leave the others alone. Reiho's done nothing, and won't act against you. Take me if you want, but leave him."

"No," Reiho said. "I'll stand with you, Lydee."

—We must fight— Marellon thought. Lydee shook her head. —You can't just give in—

"We'll be merciful," Silla said. "If you don't fight, we'll give you a quick and gentle death. You won't suffer." Lydee sensed the impatience of those around Silla.

Reiho came to Lydee's side. "It's over," he muttered

in their own tongue. "We can't fight them alone, and we can't let others risk their lives on our account." His jaw tightened. "At least we won't have to struggle with these ignorant fools and their cursed ways."

She took his hand. Anger welled up inside her; she was afraid that if she released it, her rage would wash over the village in a boiling torrent. Turning toward Marellon, she said, "You must promise me not to fight. This isn't your battle. You mustn't die because of me."

—But— the boy began to object.

"Swear that you won't, all of you. Swear it by that God of yours. I don't want such a thing on my conscience. You think your God is merciful to those who do the right thing. Maybe your deity will even accept an unbeliever if her actions spare others." She tried to give the words some conviction.

"Then we won't act, if that is what you wish." Marellon's brown eyes glistened; Luret was choking back tears.

Do they actually care for me so much? Lydee asked herself. Have I grown to love them? She supposed that she had in her own way, but her emotions still seemed pallid next to theirs. Luret's warm feelings of friendship could bind one tightly; Marellon's restrained desire often made him seem feverish. She could offer them compassion and some understanding; she had little else to give. No, that was not quite right; she would be giving her life, and maybe that would make up for what she could not offer. Her anger faded, replaced by a cold determination.

"Swear that none of you will try to help me no matter what happens," Lydee said.

—We swear— Marellon thought; the words throbbed with pain. Nenla stared at the ground as Kal's arm encircled her. Daiya rested her head against her pole.

Still clutching Reiho's hand, Lydee faced Silla. "Take us, then," she said firmly. "But don't expect it to be easy. I'll resist you, and if I die, you'll feel every moment of my death with me."

Wiland backed away. —I'll have no part of this— the young man thought. —If she had wanted to bring evil to the village, she would have allowed her friends there to fling themselves upon us and watched as we destroyed ourselves—

"Fool!" Silla shouted. "I'll fight them even if I must do it alone."

Lydee had her mental shield up before Silla could strike; it trembled under the crowd's assault. Her link burned. She fortified her shield and drew closer to Reiho's mind. If she bore the brunt of the crowd's blows, she might be able to drain their strength and spare her mentor.

—No— Reiho was thinking as he built a wall around her. —Let me save you—

—Don't fight me now— Her wall was weakening; she drew more power, wondering how long she could hold out. Silla's mind howled; needles pricked Lydee's nerves. A beast, as black as space, began to take shape in the road; its red eyes glowed as claws formed under its shapeless body. Each claw was a villager's mind, ready to rend and tear. Lydee cried out at the sight; her fear was cracking her wall. Another mind touched hers; Wiland was trying to fortify her wall, and she remembered that he had not sworn an oath with the others. She thrust his mind away.

The creature isn't really there, she told herself. The beast flickered for a moment, then roared. The sound was a blow; Lydee fell to the ground. Reiho was kneeling, hands on his ears as he buttressed his wall.

The beast undulated toward her, rearing as it struck; a claw slashed her. Lydee clutched her chest; her hand was wet. Blood oozed from a wound near her ribs, staining her tunic as the beast reached inside her, squeezing her heart and lungs. The crowd was winning; they had wounded her by turning her mind's strength against her. At that thought, her wall collapsed. She struggled for breath.

—Stop— a man's mind cried.

The beast disappeared. Lydee gasped; her heart was racing. Reiho's thoughts enclosed her as he tried to stanch the flow of blood.

—Stop. What are you doing?— Harel was running toward his partner. A whip of light flashed out from the crowd, striking Harel and knocking him to the ground.

"Stop," Harel cried aloud.

Lydee gathered the shards of her fractured mind. Harel threw up his hands as the whip danced over his shoulders; Wiland was trying to shield him. Lydee formed a mental blade; before she could stop herself, the blade slashed toward Silla.

The woman was suddenly in the air, screaming as she flew toward a hut. She crashed against the bricks and slid to the ground as Lydee watched, horrified at what she had done to Silla. The crowd was still, its walls up; one man covered his face.

Lydee struggled to her feet and stumbled toward Silla, unable to sense her sister's thoughts. The crowd parted, letting her pass. She had meant only to save Harel. Now I've killed, she thought; now I'm a murderer.

—Murderer— the crowd echoed with the beast's voice.

"Silence!" Harel shouted, walling them in with Wiland's aid; a few turned away, abandoning the battle.

Lydee dropped next to Silla, reaching out with a mental strand. Her sister's mind was failing. She clung to the wispy thoughts as they threatened to escape her grasp, then thrust her mind inside Silla's.

She was in a long, dark tunnel, being pulled rapidly toward a speck of light; Silla was dying. Her speed increased, the light drawing her on even as Lydee tried to pull back. Silla was not even trying to live.

—Leave me— a voice said feebly.

—I won't let you die— Lydee's mind answered.
—I won't let you go— With all her strength, she
resisted, holding Silla's fading thoughts as tightly as
she could. The distant light was growing larger; only
a thin thread still bound Lydee to her own body. Silla
would claim her life after all.

Lydee held on as darkness swept over her and drowned
her mind.

She blinked. A dark shape loomed over her, outlined
by the blue sky; it dropped to her side, and she made
out Marellon's face. Luret was next to him, eyes wide
with concern; Wiland stood behind her.

Lydee groaned, then felt her chest. The bleeding
had stopped; she could not find her wound. Marellon
eased her up with one strong arm. Her head swam as
she leaned against him.

—Silla— she thought, barely able to project the
name. "I didn't mean to."

—Silla's alive— the boy answered, propping her up
against the wall of the hut. At her right, she now saw,
Harel and Kal were ministering to Silla, wiping her
brow. —She's weak— Marellon continued, —and
some bones are broken, but you brought her back.
She'll be well—

"I tried to kill her."

—You didn't mean to. Even Silla will see that. And
you could have let her die, but you didn't—

The crowd had dispersed. Harel and Kal lifted Silla gently and carried her toward Kal's hut, supporting her outstretched body with their minds. Daiya and Nenla followed them inside. Reiho watched them, then came over to Lydee.

"Maybe I should have let her die," she said harshly as her mentor sat down. "She'll probably curse me for saving her." She lowered her head, appalled at her words. "Listen to me. Now I've wished for another's death. This world has made a savage of me."

—No— Marellon thought, nudging her gently with his mind. —You spared one who wanted your death and struck her only to save another—

—You have shown me my mistake— Wiland said, lowering his lids over his dark eyes. —You offered your own life for Luret's. I'm still afraid to reach out to you, for your mind feels cold and strange, but at least now I am restored to the one who loves me. We'll share what little time is left—

"You are truly my friends," Lydee said. "I don't know if my friends on the Wanderer would have offered to defend me as you did."

Marellon's head drooped. —You may be saying that only because you may never see your home again—

Reiho stood up, shading his eyes as he gazed out at the field. His mouth dropped open. "What is that?" he asked, pointing. Luret rose, covering a cheek with one hand. "Out there. Do you see?" His voice broke on the last word as his fear chilled the air.

Marellon helped Lydee to her feet. Beyond the field, small, dark shapes moved on the plain's horizon. She squinted, trying to focus. A long line of people was moving toward them. Many rode in carts; others were leading horses weighed down with sacks and bags.

Lydee hung on to Marellon's arm. "Other Earth-folk," she said, picking up the boy's thoughts. "They're coming for us. They've come for us at last."

12

Thousands of Earthfolk had converged on the village, setting up camp outside the force field. To the south, east, and north, encampments bordered the fields; in the west, another group had dug in on the other side of the river.

Their tents had become sails lifting in the wind as the invaders began to pitch them; then they had turned into birds fluttering large wings. Soon, a field of tents had covered the land, some of them elaborate and colorful pavilions of cloth, others little more than hides held up by poles. Riders on horseback, clothed in leather leggings and vests, rode at the edges of the fields; the legs of their mounts were hidden by clouds of dust. People in loincloths and beads had formed a line to the south and were carrying water from the river in buckets. The village was under seige.

—They'll win— Lydee said to Marellon as they walked along the village's perimeter, gazing out at the invaders; already the Earthfolk were harvesting what was left in the fields. —They've come to watch us die—

—Their food might give out before ours—

—I don't think so— Reiho said from behind them; he was walking with Luret and Wiland. —All they need to do is wait until we're weak and can't fight. If they need more food, they can send out hunting parties, and the river will provide water. They can wait and then take us with little risk to themselves—

They came to the riverbank and leaned against the force field, staring at the opposite shore. Several small children were splashing in the shallows, as if the seige were only an outing and a chance to play. Adults lingered near the young ones, gazing suspiciously toward the village. Wiland made a fist with his right hand and struck his left palm.

The atmosphere of the village had changed after the shock and dismay of seeing its enemies approach had passed. The sullenness, passivity, and despair had been dispelled, replaced by a nervous anxiety and even some anticipation of a last battle. The waiting was over. Other villagers were gathering along the wall, watching to see what would happen now.

The Earthfolk had been arriving all day. Lydee supposed that, in the distance, others were still arriving. It seemed as if all Earth was coming to pass judgment, though that couldn't be possible; those on other continents would not have been able to make the journey. It hardly mattered. Those far away had probably linked their thoughts in a long chain connecting them to those outside in order to witness the battle; the village would face the combined force of thousands of minds. It would not be a battle but a slaughter.

—Daiya still believes we'll be saved— Luret thought.

—Daiya is wrong— Lydee replied.

—You're not frightened—

Lydee shook her head. —No, I'm not. It seems easier to be frightened when you think there's something you can do. It's out of our hands now— She glanced at Reiho, whose fear had crystallized; it was turning his mind into a glassy network of ice that she could barely stand to touch.

—Perhaps the Minds will help us now— Luret said.

—The Minds— Wiland responded. —The Minds might have kept them away in the first place, yet They did nothing—

Lydee walked toward a field, gazing out across the meadow to the hill where Daiya's old hut still stood. Earthfolk on blankets perched along the slopes, and she noticed that the shuttle had been dragged toward the meadow. A few people were running their hands over its sides; a door opened and they jumped away, pointing and waving their hands. The door closed. Several gray-haired people eyed the shuttle from a distance; one was shaking his head. Had they known how to work the synthesizer, they could have supplied themselves with food indefinitely while waiting for the villagers to die.

—Now they'll know that someone unlike them is here— Lydee said to the others, suppressing the rest of her thoughts. That alone would be enough to condemn the village.

At dusk, the villagers began to carry their tables out of their huts, setting them up in a circle just inside the invisible wall. Torches were lighted and planted in the ground as the village prepared for its last feast. Spits holding the bodies of pigs and fowl turned as minds directed the heat at the roasting meat.

—Bring the food— Cerwen ordered, and men and women carried platters to the tables. —Bring the wine. Let those outside see that we are ready to welcome our fate— His thoughts and those of the other Merging Selves were serene. The villagers had always held feasts before sending their young people out to face their ordeals; it had seemed only proper that they should celebrate before undergoing this last ordeal. No one had objected to Cerwen's proposal. They would have their feast and die unafraid instead of wasting away in front of their enemies.

Lydee sat at one table, trying to ignore the odor of

meat. The villagers had slaughtered the animals gently, careful not to cause pain, yet each death had seemed a precursor of the human deaths that would soon follow. Lydee and Reiho, sickened, had been forced to keep up their walls. Two of the village cats crouched at her feet, snarling at each other over a piece of meat on the ground.

The field outside the wall was reddened by the setting sun. A few fires burned in the encampment; men and women stood at the edge of the field, watching the village. She lifted her head defiantly, then turned toward Reiho, who was seated at her left. He nibbled at a few grapes while eyeing his wine cup dubiously.

—Drink it— she said. —You needn't worry about it making you sick now— He grimaced. —I wish I could believe what the Earthpeople do— she continued.

Reiho sipped his wine. —I'm glad now that I don't believe such things. I don't have to fear punishment, and I won't be rewarded. There's only the darkness. If you look at it that way, it's almost comforting. At least we won't have to struggle on. I can always hope that somehow our friends on the Wanderer will learn from what's happened here—

—What could they possibly learn from this? That people are capable of killing others who seem different, or who doubt? That doesn't seem much of a lesson—

—Perhaps they'll learn that life isn't something to

be wasted and frittered away. We have everything we want. These people have almost nothing, and yet their lives have a purpose. They see death all the time, and maybe that heightens the few joys they do have. We keep real life, along with death, at a distance— He paused, collecting his thoughts. —The cometdwellers are in part responsible for what's happened here. We rejected our past and forgot, just as the people here did. We hid from Earth. We might have come back sooner. If we had—

—Might— Daiya interrupted. —If. Those words have such power for you. You pick at them and think they'll reveal some secret— She was sitting across from them, devouring a meat pie with grim determination. —I refuse to accept death until the moment comes. Until then, I'll hope, and so should you—

—We'll feast— Kal said, reaching for a corn cake. —Tomorrow, we'll hurl our minds at the wall, and as we weaken, we'll die. And even if we manage to open it, those outside will strike us down. That's all that can happen, cousin. This is our last night in this life—

Daiya finished her pie and took a sip of wine. —They could have destroyed us from a distance— she said. —They didn't have to come here and wait outside— She glanced at Marellon as he set a bowl of fruit on the table and sat down at Lydee's right. —I've been watching them. We can't touch their minds, and yet I feel as though I have. I think they're afraid—

—How can they fear us?— Luret asked as Nenla handed her a bowl of soup.

—Maybe they have their own doubts— Daiya reached for a peach. —Maybe they disagree. They put up a wall, but did not strike. They enclosed us here, but did not crush us. Now they have seen that vessel outside, and they must know that none of us could have built it. And they do not know what powers our visitors might have—

Lydee nibbled at a carrot. She was eating without tasting the food; her throat tightened as she swallowed.

Daiya still hoped. Her face brightened, as if a light were shining inside her. A tendril of her mind brushed against Lydee; Lydee reached out to Reiho. Soon those at the table were linked in a chain touching all of the villagers. Nenla gazed out at the encampment and laughed, throwing her head back. A blond young man at the next table lifted his cup; his mind was filled with chants and prayers. The wine had gone to Lydee's head; she wondered if she was sensing her own drunkenness or someone else's.

—I could leave this world willingly— Silla was saying, —if I knew you cared for me— She was sitting with Harel at one end of the table, her head bound by a cloth. Her right arm was in a sling; her injured leg, dressed in a splint, rested on her partner's lap. —But I know Daiya still draws you—

Harel shook his head. —What I love in you is what

I love in her. How can I separate those feelings? I've never betrayed you, Silla, and neither has she. I was wrong to hide part of myself from you— He leaned closer to her, weaving their minds together as he tried to help his partner heal more quickly.

Lydee withdrew, walling herself in for a moment. Their resolutions, she thought cynically, would never be tested, so it was easy to make promises. These people drew together only for death; if rescue were suddenly offered to them, they would resume their bickering before long. Even Reiho had fallen under the spell, hoping to find a purpose in his approaching extinction. She no longer felt the hope Daiya had conveyed. Reaching for her cup, she emptied it and poured herself more wine.

Nenla and Kal leaned against each other. Luret had left the table and was communing with Wiland, who turned toward Lydee. —The Merged One might accept your soul— he thought gently. —We may be blessed, for we only tried to do what was right. The coming ordeal will purge us of sin and prepare us for the next life— He scowled. —And those outside will be punished for their crime—

—No, Wiland— Luret said as she took his arm. —You must not wish for that—

Lydee finished a piece of bread, then got up and walked toward the force field. The sun had set; fires flickered in the encampment. A family to her right was dancing, arms linked as they hummed a wordless song. Other villagers were entering huts.

—Lydee— Marellon was approaching her; she turned to face him. —I must ask you this now, because there is not much time left— His mind was drawn tight, a string about to break. She waited. He looked down, poking at the ground with his toes.

—Ask me anything you like— she said, trying to ease his embarrassment.

—Will you be my partner?— The words tumbled from his mind. —I'll ask for nothing of you except the pledge—

Her mind swelled; she took a breath. Her joy had disoriented her; she had nearly agreed. —Marellon— She tried to collect her thoughts.

—You have grown to feel something for me. I see it now—

She could not deny it. —This is new for me— she responded. —I don't know how to answer you. If we die, we cannot be partners. If we live, I may not be able to keep the promise— Even though she had tried to mute her thoughts, she sensed his pain and regretted the answer.

—I'll pledge myself to you, then— he said. —You may do as you wish, but I'll have no other partner—

—You're young, Marellon. Your feelings run high and you believe that now, but later you would forget me and find another partner, and you would wonder

at your impulsiveness. Don't promise yourself to me
only to find that you must break the promise later—

—You seem to think we'll live—

—No. I don't know. We skydwellers are so used to
thinking of death as something we choose, something
that won't often come upon us against our will—

—If you live, you'll go back to your world—

She looked up at the comet. —Yes. But I won't
forget you—

—You will. Earth will seem very far away—

She took his arm. —How foolish we are, Marellon.
We're arguing about something that will never come
to pass, most likely— They walked alongside the wall.
Their enemies, who should have been celebrating their
approaching victory, were hiding in their tents while
the doomed village danced and sang.

She thought of Home. Would her friends there mourn
her? Homesmind would quickly ease their sorrow. When
the cometdwellers learned of her fate, and Reiho's,
they would reject the mindpowers Homesmind could
give them. She could already hear the arguments. Such
abilities would shatter the customs that had kept their
world peaceful; with their inner feelings so open to
others, the cometdwellers might even come to fight
one another as the Earthfolk had. Her short life, and
Reiho's, would be no more than a ripple in the sea,
altering nothing.

Marellon stopped and took her gently by the elbows.

Half of his face was shadowed, the other half lighted by a nearby torch. —It isn't true— he thought. —You've changed me. I once looked at you with loathing, seeing one alien to me, but now I can touch your mind and know you for what you are. Daiya has her lost sister back, and Silla and Harel have healed themselves—

—That is nothing. I touched a few small lives, and my own has changed, and it'll come to nothing when we die—

—You're wrong, Lydee. Touching other lives during the short time we have—why, it's all we've ever had, isn't it?—

She gazed into his eyes. His face had changed; his features seemed finer. Perhaps his face had always looked that way, brave and intelligent instead of hard and coarse, and she had simply been unable to see it.

—I'll make a pledge, Marellon. But I make it only until we meet our fate. If we live, I won't hold you to it. It would be easy for me to say that I would be your partner always, but it would be a false promise, and you would know that. I can't die with a lie between us—

—Then that is what I'll promise you, Lydee. Even that's more than you're accustomed to giving—

—Let's go inside—

His mind warmed as he read her intention. Together, they walked back to his sister's hut.

*   *   *

Lydee opened her eyes. Marellon slept at her side. They were still alone; she supposed that the others were saying farewell to friends.

She gazed at the boy next to her, still feeling as though he had left part of his mind inside her. His love had been strong and heartfelt, almost frightening her with its intensity, yet she had welcomed it, seeing herself through Marellon's eyes as he embraced her mind. The feeling she had once called love now seemed a frail sensation, an emotion so easily given to others that it was hardly a gift at all.

She rose carefully, not wanting to disturb him, and crossed the room to the doorway, peering outside. Reiho looked up; he was sitting on the ground, back against the hut. At his side, Daiya slept on a blanket. Outside the invisible wall, the encampment was awake; a few people were forming a line in the field. Their waiting would soon be over.

She loved Marellon; she knew that now, and at last understood why Earthfolk made their pledges. He had seen more of her mind than she had ever shown to anyone, and she wanted to explore his, but they would never have the time. Marellon, at least, would die content, secure in her love; she would never have the chance to disappoint him. She shivered; she did not want him to die at all.

Villagers were leaving their huts, filing toward the

riverbank, where they were to gather by the wall. "It's time," she said to Reiho in their own tongue.

His eyes widened for a moment. "I know." He straightened his shoulders. "You had better wake the boy." He scowled. "We shall all sleep soon enough."

As she and Marellon came to the riverbank, Lydee saw that several families were kneeling in prayer, while others had their arms locked in embraces. Tears ran down the faces of a few young people as their parents or friends sought to comfort them. Wiland had his arms around the shoulders of an older woman whose black eyes resembled his.

Leito approached, then took Lydee's hand. —Farewell, Granddaughter. I am sorry you had to come to this— Leito's son Vasen was holding on to Kal with one pudgy hand; Nenla clung to another old woman, stroking her silver hair.

—I wish I could have helped— Lydee said. Leito let go and went to Cerwen, who had gathered several Merging Selves around him.

—It is time— the old man called out. —Those beyond will see us die bravely and know that we are not evil. We shall hurl our minds at the wall until the Merged One claims us at last—

Lydee felt numb. Luret s eyes were pieces of green glass; she did not look at Wiland as he joined her. Lydee strengthened her mind, then tugged at the sleeves of her silver suit. She had put the garment back on, shedding her tunic and pants; Reiho also was clothed in silver. Let them see what we are, she thought as she gazed at the encampment across the river. She and Reiho, being the strongest, would likely be the last to die. She tried not to think of that.

Cerwen tugged at the Net, binding them all as they drew power.

—It is not time— Daiya protested. —The Minds said They would save us. Let Them come to our aid now—

—We are abandoned— the Merging Selves whispered.

—They must help us— Daiya said.

The villagers hesitated. Flickers of hope warmed the strands of the Net. Images were forming along the bank. The people across the river threw up their hands as the images took shape; others retreated toward the tents.

—Brun— Daiya thought as her father appeared; a female form sprang up beside him. —Anra—

Other specters appeared, lining the banks; the villagers wailed. —The dead are with us— Cerwen thought. —They have come to claim us—

—No, not to claim you— a thousand ghostly voices replied. —It is not yet your time. Remember this: The energy of the Minds under the mountains is yours. Guard yourselves. Do not seek to do evil, and you will live—

On the other side of the river, people huddled near

one another as others, running along the bank, tried to rally them. Horses reared as their masters struggled to hold their reins.

/We are with you/ This voice was resonant; Lydee could sense its power.

—The Minds— Daiya said. —They've spoken at last—

/We are ready to help you now/ The voice was dispassionate, but there was an undercurrent of sorrow. /Remember that your strength lies in protecting yourselves, not in striking out/

The crowd of ghostly images disappeared, yet Lydee felt that other minds were still with them, lending their strength. She stared out at the river, wondering if even the Minds could help them against so many.

A wall of flame was suddenly in front of the villagers; a crack of thunder slapped their ears. The fire licked at their feet. Lydee covered her eyes as the wall fell. A strong wind washed over them, then died.

It was time to confront their enemies.

13

The villagers waited. The Merging Selves lined up along the edge of the river and faced their antagonists, who still had not struck.

Across the river, twenty old people were gathering along the bank, waving other Earthfolk away. One old man wore only beads and a loincloth, while another was dressed in a long, striped robe; two of the women wore leather leggings and high, fringed boots.

—Truce— several minds called out. The villagers nodded, assenting.

One woman stepped forward. Her white hair was tied back with a leather thong; a beaded belt circled her waist. Her long, brown robe fluttered around her ankles; one hand held a spear.

—I am Talah NaisVel— the old woman said as she threw down her spear. —We offer a truce only for the time it takes to communicate with you. We are the oldest Merging Selves of several villages, and we shall speak for everyone here. All other minds are shielded so that your separateness does not stain them, and so that the eager among us do not strike at you before we are ready. If you attempt to lash out at us, we'll wall you in again— She paused. Some of the younger people behind her glanced nervously from side to side. —Who will speak for you—

—I shall— Cerwen replied. —I am Cerwen IviaRey. You have your truce for now. We do not wish harm to come to you. If you search our minds, you'll see that—

—You are great sinners— Talah said. —You seek to trick us with your illusions and to lead all of Earth into wickedness. When you reached out to us, before we saw what you had become, we learned that your Net was torn by separateness. Your faith was shaken, and your thoughts carried visions of separate souls that had not died but lived on in a far place. You questioned custom, and yet your doubts only brought you misery. Even then, we did not crush you, for we were afraid of the strange power we felt from you. Instead, we walled you in so that the evil could not infect us—

—It was not only our power you felt— Cerwen answered, —but also that of the Minds humanity built in past ages— Talah tensed at his words. —They are mighty machines that are the source of all the power we have. For a long time, They slept because we did not use most of Their power, but now They have awakened and speak. They were built to serve us. They will wither away if we don't reach out to Them now, and all our powers will wither away with Them—

The woman threw up a hand. —What evil is this? Only God can give us our powers, and yet you say machines did. Do you think we can accept such a blasphemy?—

—You may touch those Minds yourself. They lie under the mountains yonder and in other far places, cloaked in pillars and hidden from our sight. Without Them, we would all be locked inside ourselves—

Talah shook her head. —It cannot be true, yet I see you believe it and mistake an illusion for truth—

—God gave us our powers— Cerwen said. —The machines built in past times have given us the use of these powers. Can that be a blasphemy?—

—Those long ago were separate from the world. They reached for too much and destroyed themselves. Now you will dream of doing the same—

Cerwen bowed his head. —I, too, believed that once. For many cycles we have tormented ourselves, unable either to accept this new knowledge or to return to old ways. Some of us came to believe that we were cursed. But we cannot turn from truth. We seek only to share what we have learned. We believed that all human beings lived on Earth and that those born as separate selves had no souls. We thought that only those like us lived. Now we know that people live in the sky, and that their ancestors and ours were the same, and that separate souls can be linked to us—

—Don't speak such evil— Talah objected.

—Two separate selves are here— Cerwen gestured at Lydee and Reiho. —This man and this girl are separate selves—

—I see no man— Talah was staring directly at Reiho. —I see no girl—

—You must make an effort to see them as they are and not as your mind shows them to you. The man's home is the comet that lights the sky—

—An evil omen—

—No, only a place where men and women live. The girl is from the comet also, but she was born here in this village as a solitary and was given to the sky-dwellers. Separate selves, yet they mindspeak and can sense your words. They can find a way to help other separate selves do the same—

—That cannot be—

—It's true— Cerwen replied. —Solitaries are not without powers. It is only that their powers are too weak for us to sense and must be strengthened. That is what these skydwellers have shown us—

Several of the old people across the river were shaking their heads in dismay; Talah clasped her hands together. —Then you are saying that every time we've taken the life of a solitary, we have robbed a body of its soul—

—We once did the same. That girl is my granddaughter. Had the skydwellers not taken her, she would have died, and I would have committed a sin without knowing it—

Talah gazed at Lydee, who could sense the woman's hatred. Marellon drew closer to her while Luret and Wiland stepped forward as if ready to defend her. —I see only beings of metal and wire, living matter entwined with machines. You've conjured up an illusion—

—Touch their minds— Cerwen said. —Look at them only with your eyes and you'll see that they have our form. Search their vessel by the hill. Do you think we can dream such a thing?— He paused for a moment. —Why are you here? If you wished, you could have destroyed us without traveling so far, or walled us in and let us die—

—You must know— Talah shook a fist. —You drew us here with your visitations. We have seen our dead and have heard their voices and knew that you must have sent such illusions to plague us. Somehow, you breached our wall. You tore its fabric, and we struck back, and then you sent us ghosts in order to drive us mad—

Cerwen held out his hands in bewilderment. —But we have not sent anything—

—Who else could have sent them? The dead walked among us and spoke evil words, saying that we had been living in illusion and ignorance, and tempting us to doubt. It was then that we knew we had to confront you—

—But we sent nothing. It must have been the Minds Who spoke to you, as They spoke to us. Look into my mind, Talah NaisVel. Then you'll understand—

—Deceiver! Don't open your mind to me—

The old man in the loincloth squatted on the bank. —You speak of impossible things— he thought. —You show us two shining creatures and call them people. Yet I can sense no evil intent inside you— He glanced up at Talah. —Perhaps we should withdraw and reconsider—

—Silence, Keshal— Talah glared down at him. —Already they sow dissension among us— She turned toward her companions, throwing a mental shield around them as they communed.

The villagers sat down, waiting. Lydee wrapped her arms around her legs. If the Mindcores had indeed sent images to the other Earthfolk, then They were responsible for bringing them here. She rested her chin on her knees. The Minds had not saved Anra and Brun; They might allow many to die.

Talah turned toward them again. —Heed these

words— she thought fiercely. —We shall give you a choice— She pointed at Lydee and Reiho. —Destroy these illusions and swear to return to the right way. If you do, you will be spared. It is evil for people to war among themselves as Earth did long ago, and we will show mercy if you repent. Give up your sin. Allow us to search your minds to be sure of your sincerity, and prove it to us by destroying the monsters you harbor—

Reiho stood up and pulled Lydee to her feet.

—No— Marellon replied as he moved in front of Lydee.

—No— Luret and Wiland said together.

—No— Harel responded. Even Silla, seated next to him on a stretcher of leather and wood, was shaking her head.

—No— Daiya said, taking a step forward, then wincing; her leg had not completely healed. —It was I who brought them here, so you will have to take me, too— Others villagers stepped forward with her. —You say it is evil for people to war with one another, yet you want to harm two who came to us in friendship—

—You cannot have them— Cerwen said. —I see that we are all agreed on that. Even those who have feared them will not turn them over to you or take their lives. We are united at last and cannot turn from the truth, however harsh it is—

—Then you will die— Talah's mind screamed,

—and the Merged One will refuse to accept your souls. I curse you, Cerwen IviaRey, you and all of your people— She picked up her spear, stepped back, and raised her arms.

A dark storm cloud formed overhead. Lightning struck the ground near Lydee; she leaped back. The cloud lengthened, becoming a funnel. Several villagers jumped up and began to run toward their huts.

—Draw together— Daiya called out to them. —Link minds. We must draw on the power of the Minds to protect us. Hold to Them— The fleeing people halted and wheeled around.

Lydee tugged at the bonds of the village's Net, then directed her mind at the whirling storm as she shielded herself. The cloud broke apart, showering them with rain as it was dispersed. Reiho was straining, drawing on power to shield those around him.

Wiland glared at the old people across the river; Lydee read his intention. —No— Luret thought, trying to restrain him. —You mustn't strike out at them. We can't win that way— The young man was draining her strength as she bound his mind. —They've shielded themselves—

Lydee could now sense walls around the minds of the invaders, too strong to be overcome. Their enemies did not need to launch an overwhelming attack; they could simply wait as the village weakened while continuing to jab at the villagers intermittently. A tongue of fire flashed before her, licking her arm; the pain nearly made her lose her shield. She stared at her arm in shock as Reiho fed her some of his power; her sleeve had been singed black.

—They're not that strong— Daiya cried out to the village. —So many people should be stronger. Their shield is firm, but brittle. They are struggling even as they try to strike— Lydee sensed the rest of Daiya's thoughts; the Earthfolk were wasting power and were still tired from their journey. Their advantage was not as great as it seemed.

She probed the walls around the beseigers, touching a weak spot. She drew back. A young man in a leather cloak was running toward Talah, arms out as if pleading with her; she thrust him away with her mind and he sprawled among the reeds near the shore.

—We must strike at them— Wiland thought; others were signaling their agreement. —If we don't reduce their numbers, we'll have no chance—

—No— Lydee responded. —Use your strength to protect yourself— A fiery claw appeared, grasping at Wiland; Lydee lashed it away.

—The Minds have said we must not do evil— Daiya said. —We must use our power to protect ourselves and parry their blows, not to kill—

The Merging Selves across the river were retreating from the bank, climbing up to a small rise above it. Lydee drew more power, surprised that she still could.

The Net trembled as one mind dropped out. Harel knelt next to Silla, shielding his unconscious partner with his mental wall.

The water on the other side of the river began to boil, seething with the encampment's rage, then rose, becoming a vast, gray wall; fish leaped from its side. The wall of water swept toward the village as the villagers threw their minds against the wave. The water hung over them, perilously near, then fell away, drenching those nearest the bank.

The air rippled as beasts took shape on the water, screaming for blood as they showed ivory teeth. One young woman near Luret screamed in terror; claws ripped at her chest before others could shield her. She lay in the reeds, her pale eyes blinking one last time as she died; a thread of the Net snapped.

The villagers buttressed their shields and their Net as they shook under isolated blows. The beasts flickered out. A few invaders had fainted, and others were dragging them back toward the tents. The Earthfolk were hurling their minds at the villagers instead of waiting them out.

Lydee heard the sound of thunder; the ground under her feet shook. A woman screamed.

"The horses!" Marellon cried aloud.

She turned. Her throat locked, cutting off her cry. A herd of horses was stampeding toward them from the field nearby, their hooves beating the ground.

The Net broke. Villagers lifted themselves, wasting their energy as they sought safety on nearby roofs. One boy fell, struck down by his terror; a man leaned over him helplessly.

—Hold the Net— Daiya commanded. —Keep up your shields—

Reiho began to run toward the horses; Lydee hurried after him. As the beasts bore down on them, eyes rolling as their nostrils flared, the two hurled a wall of air with all their might.

The horses screamed and whinnied as they struck the invisible barrier; a few fell in the river and were swept away by the rapids. One white horse fell at Lydee's feet, narrowly missing her with one flailing hoof, then struggled up from the mud and trotted on along the bank. Other horses veered off, racing on through the village streets.

—Hold to the Net— Cerwen said.

The village regrouped along the bank, strengthening the Net. Lydee stumbled back, hanging on to Reiho. Her strength was now nearly gone, and her mentor was weaker. Leito knelt next to two old people who lay on the ground, unable to move.

—The Minds have lied— a tall, curly-haired man cried out. —We are lost. Let's at least avenge ourselves before we die— A woman near him seized him with her mind, holding him back.

Across the river, Talah and her companions were

huddled together; one old man shook his fist. As she gazed at them, Lydee felt her strength returning, flowing into her in a clear, steady stream.

Marellon grabbed her arm. —Do you feel it?— he asked as they continued to shield themselves; the assault had subsided and their walls no longer shook with mental blows. —All that strength. Somehow, the Minds under the mountains are giving us what we need. We shouldn't have been able to shield ourselves for so long—

—Even the Minds can't help us when our bodies fail— she replied. So far the village had kept its advantage only because its enemies could not accept the existence of the Mindcores and therefore were not drawing on the power available to them. But the villagers could not hold out for much longer.

She reached out, sensing the hatred of the encampment; their shield had grown weak enough to allow her to touch their minds. —Listen to me— she called out to Talah. —We must stop this battle. Look inside me and see what I am—

—Don't!— Marellon cried as Reiho tried to shield her.

—I must speak to them. Maybe then they'll understand—

—Shield yourself— Marellon answered.

Talah lifted her spear, pointing it at Lydee. —Aim your minds at that creature— she ordered. —It must have taught them one of its evil arts to make them so strong. Destroy that monster and its fellow, and we'll have our victory—

Lydee threw up her wall, making it so tight that she could no longer hear any thoughts, then entwined her mental tendrils with Reiho's. A vise gripped her head; her skull would be crushed. Blood trickled from her nose. The pain disappeared as villagers lent her their strength, but her link in their chain was failing.

"Help me," she whispered. The Net was slipping away. Her arms flailed about as the vise pressed her again. The village's Merging Selves were weakening; the Net shook as several more dropped away. Reiho held his head, his face contorted with pain.

The vise broke. Talah collapsed; other bodies lay around her. A younger woman picked up the spear. "Enough!" she screamed at the top of her voice.

Lydee opened her mind cautiously.

—Enough— the woman said again. —Their minds resist, but there are other ways to die— She pointed toward the multitudes in the village's fields. —We must now turn to the ways of old Earth. Gather your knives and spears and arrows and go among the evildoers, slaying them with your weapons. They cannot resist all of us, and however many of us fall in the fight, there will be others to take their place. Kill them as you would your cattle and sheep—

—We cannot— several minds replied.

Lydee turned. A group stood on the other side of a ditch, several paces from the villagers on the bank.

—We have fought enough— the group continued. —We strike at them and still they do not reach out to harm us. Is that the way of evildoers?—

—Heed my words— the woman with the spear said.

—Heed ours— A small, dark woman in hides stepped out from the group near the ditch. —They spoke of Minds in machines that can give us power we've never used—

—You should not have heard that. You young ones were to shield yourselves—

—I'll hear what I please. They spoke of those Minds. Haven't they shown it is true? If it were not, wouldn't we have been able to destroy them by now?—

—It is false— the older woman replied.

—You ask us to go among them. Many of us will die as well. I will not slaughter fellow human beings—

—They are not that. They have wandered from truth and are now lower than the separate selves we bury at birth—

—I have begun to doubt— the small woman said. —I have looked at those creatures there with my eyes, not with my mind, and I can see now that they wear a human shape— She gestured at Reiho and Lydee. —I do not know where they come from, but they can touch our thoughts. It is the duty of all minds to draw closer, and yet we turn from these people and seek their deaths. I think it is we who have been lost to evil.

You say that we must lay hands on them in violence. I can't do that—

—Nor can I— someone else thought.

—Nor I—

—I cannot—

—You would attack with your minds— the older woman across the river cried, —yet you shrink from using your hands. What nonsense is that?—

—I won't strike at them in either way again— the small woman answered. Groups of invaders were retreating, scurrying toward their tents; others waved their spears and knives in frustration.

—Fools— the Merging Selves on the other side of the river screamed in unison. —Then you, too, will die—

The young woman dropped to the ground, shielding her mind as others fell around her. The ground began to shake as the encampment fought; a crack appeared near the ditch. The river overran its banks, lapping at the feet of the Merging Selves on the rise. Tents tilted, then collapsed, looking like alighting birds with outstretched wings.

"They're fighting among themselves," Lydee said aloud. Luret covered her eyes. "We have to stop them."

"How?" Wiland asked, heedless of the shallow water now covering his feet. "They'll use their strength against one another, and perhaps they'll have little left to deal with us."

Luret looked up; her face was immobile. Across the

field, men and women were shielding their children with their bodies as others came at them with knives. Luret darted away, auburn curls bobbing as she ran toward the field. Wiland hesitated, then hurried after her.

Lydee felt sick. A bitter taste filled her mouth; she leaned over, about to retch.

—Stop— Daiya called to those across the river. —You mustn't do this— Villagers were already running across the fields, lending their strength to those trying to defend themselves. Nenla threw herself across one child; a man about to stab suddenly staggered back. Leito was leading a group of women toward the meadow.

Lydee stumbled toward the ditch. A man held a spear over the small, dark woman, freezing as the woman restrained him with her mind. Lydee leaped to her side, knocking the man aside with one arm, then parried a blow from a muscular young woman. Where were the Minds? They could stop this slaughter, yet They were silent.

—Help us— Daiya was demanding. —Help us now. Many will die if you don't— Other villagers joined the cry. —Help us. Speak to them—

—Help us— several invaders joined in.

The air began to sparkle, glistening with specks of light. The small woman climbed to her feet, clinging to Lydee as Reiho leaped over the ditch to their side. The village was surrounded by tiny, twinkling stars. A moan went up from those on the other side of the river.

/You have forgotten Us/ The Minds were speaking; Lydee heard Their forceful voices inside her head. /You built Us, and then forgot Us. We were to be your servants, and you abandoned Us. Some of you fled from this planet while the others dreamed. You have lived in a dream for eons, using only the smallest part of what We could provide, and now We are withering away. If We die, your powers will die, too/

Talah had been revived; she was on her knees, leaning against her spear as her companions cowered around her. She raised her head. —You are an illusion— she thought. —I do not hear you. I reject you—

/You cannot reject Us. Will you turn from the truth? Hear Our words. We have waited for you to remember Us, but you do not. We can wait no longer/

Ghostly figures were taking shape around the village, becoming the transparent shapes of men, women, and children. A multitude formed in the fields; others appeared on the other side of the river. Talah cried out as the specters moved through the encampment, each embracing a person with ghostly arms. The image of a young man had risen before Talah; she warded him off before falling to the ground.

/Look at the skydwellers/ the voices continued. /Know that they also have minds like yours, and can give up their solitude/

"It's true," the small woman said aloud as she let

go of Lydee. "What will become of us now?"

A silvery ghost was forming in front of Reiho; it bore the blurred face of a boy. Reiho sighed as its arms touched him. Lydee caught her mentor as he fell; she could not sense his mind and knew that he had fainted. The ghost lifted a hand before flickering out.

A bright light shone above the village, lighting the huts and turning their roofs gold. /We shall not force Our will upon you/ the Minds whispered. /You must decide for yourselves. We can only serve, and hope for life/

The light dimmed as the ghostly people rose into the air, soaring toward the mountains. Those in the encampment began to moan, mourning their dead.

The sky was violet. Shadows had lengthened around the village as the Earthfolk went about their unhappy work; the dead had to be buried. A band of men and women across the river were lifting dirt with their minds; clouds settled around their feet as they prepared a grave for Talah and the Merging Selves who had died with her. Other people were aiding the village in burying the few who had fallen there. Some outsiders had filtered into the village, where they now sat in the shade of the huts communing with Cerwen.

Lydee had led the stunned, silent Reiho farther up the bank and now sat with him near a garden. Lumps of dirt and bits of thatching were strewn about the garden, where tiny shoots poked above ground, still clinging to life.

"The break is mended," Reiho said abruptly.

She glanced at him. He had said nothing since the end of the battle, as if the sight of the bloodshed had robbed him of the power to form words. She shivered; her hands were cold.

"The break?" she asked, unable to read his thoughts. "What do you mean?"

"I no longer feel the break separating me from my former self, the Reiho who died here. I've healed at last. Somehow—" He held out a hand, apparently unable to express himself.

She touched his mind. He was still the Reiho she knew, but she sensed the presence of a part of him she had not felt before.

"It was the shock," she said at last, "the shock of seeing what happened here."

"The image that reached out to me was my former self."

The battle had clearly unhinged him. "It was only an image, nothing more."

He sighed. "I don't know. Perhaps the ghosts are images of another probability, another plane or continuum where those people still live, and the Minds have found a way to show them to us. Or maybe the Minds know how to preserve the mental patterns of those who are gone."

"They're only the memories the Minds hold of those who lived—they cannot be more."

"All I know is that somehow I've been healed."

She felt empty. Her mind was not calm; the sight of death had not healed her. That she was alive at all was only chance.

"Look at them, Reiho." She waved a hand at the encampment. "They wanted us dead, and now they come among us. The Mindcores could have stopped it. They care nothing for us."

/Nothing?/

She looked around hastily, but no one except Reiho seemed to have heard the voice.

/What would you have had Us do?/ the Minds went on. /If We had revealed Ourselves immediately to those who came here, many more would have died, and those who lived would have crushed this village in their fright/

—There must be hundreds dead now— she thought bitterly.

/There might have been thousands. We could only aid this village while hoping that its enemies would begin to doubt their purpose and become open to Our words. Had We shown Ourselves too soon, the shock would have been too great for most of them. Those who died were not struck down by Us, but by their own inability to accept the truth. They killed themselves/

—You might have prevented it— she protested.

/We could not. Do you think We watched without suffering? Now Earth will heal/

—You kept us here. We weren't needed. Perhaps the Earthfolk would have been better off without our presence—

/You are wrong, young one/

She waited, but heard no more. Reiho nudged her; she looked up.

Five young people with black hair and coppery complexions were approaching her on horseback. They slid off the backs of their mounts and came nearer, holding the reins. Lydee rose as one girl took a step toward her.

—It is said that you are from the sky— the girl thought.

—My companion is from the sky. I lived there and was raised there, but I was born here on Earth as a solitary—

—Yet you mindspeak— the girl said.

—Yes, and all solitaries can do the same. There is a way to open their minds—

The girl tilted her head. —That would be a blessing. So many mourn the small ones who cannot live, and now we need do that no more. You will stay here, then, and provide this gift to all—

Lydee lowered her eyes. —I don't know what I'll do. But then it's not up to me. I don't know if I can go home—

—I sense that you have much to teach us and you might learn from us also—

Lydee did not reply.

—We must consider this. It goes against so much of what we've been taught— The Earthgirl paused. —Even now, our remaining Merging Selves are communicating with other villages, and all of Earth will wrestle with this truth. It will be hard for many to accept it—

The young people remounted and rode away. Other strangers stood in the road; she could feel their minds nudging at hers. She felt their sorrow, but also their hope. Slowly, she opened her mind.

14

The tents were down. Sacks had been loaded into wagons and onto the backs of horses. A few remaining Earthfolk had filed past Lydee, probing her mind and then touching her hands, reassuring themselves that she was real. Now they were shadows, retreating through the dusk, their figures blurred by the fading light. She felt bruised.

Lydee stretched, then rose. A few villagers lingered at the edges of the newly replanted fields; others were returning to their huts to prepare their evening meal. She caught a glimpse of Daiya and Reiho crossing the meadow.

Luret took her arm, startling her. "Your wall is strong," Luret said aloud.

Lydee nodded, worn out. Her mind ached from all the probing of the last few days. She had shown the Earthfolk images of her world, longing for it as she shaped the pictures of the lake, the caves, and the river while feeling the disbelief, fear, or pity of those viewing the scenes. Daiya had tried to give the strangers hope, telling them of her plans to teach those born as solitaries. Some of the Earthfolk had responded to her thoughts with desperation as they tried to make sense of what had happened, while others, still mourning their dead, seemed lost, their thoughts in turmoil. Some, she knew, would not live.

"I'm very tired," Lydee said at last.

"I understand," Luret replied. "I know it was hard for you to open your mind to so many even after the time you've spent with us. You did well. Some have already come to trust you and Reiho." She paused. "Come back to our hut tonight. Nenla and Kal won't ask you to mindspeak if you don't wish it, and Marellon will be glad to see you there. We can decide—"

"I can decide nothing. I need solitude for a while."

Luret patted her arm, then departed.

Lydee strode across the meadow toward the shuttle. The craft had been righted and now stood nearer the hill, facing the village. Next to it, a fire burned; Daiya and Reiho sat near the flames. As Lydee approached, Daiya looked up; Reiho motioned to her. She sat down next to him.

—We'll have to help other villages— Daiya was thinking. —They may struggle as we have for so long— She glanced at Lydee. —You are unhappy—

Lydee shrugged. —Your village will take you back now, and you have a purpose. But I can't share your life. I'll always be outside it. The battle's over—

—It is not over—

—It's over for me. There's nothing left for me to do here—

—But there is, Lydee. We'll need your help when more solitaries are born, as I'm sure they will be. You can teach them about your world and show that there is a bond linking all people wherever they live and whatever they are. We can't even provide those devices they need without your help—

—Homesmind can send you machines to do that, and to teach you about the links. You don't need me—

—You forget— Reiho said. —We are still unable to leave—

/You are mistaken/

Lydee started; the Minds had spoken inside all of them.

/We will not keep you here now if you do not wish it. The ordeal is past. The young Mind of your world will speak to you, and your vessel can take you there/ As They spoke, Lydee felt her channel open.

—Homesmind— she called out.

I am here, Lydee. Its voice seemed oddly mournful and weary. *At last we speak again.*

"Homesmind," she said aloud.

I am sorry I could not regain contact, though I tried. It distresses Me that I could not reach out to you and Reiho. I watched, and could do nothing. You were the eyes through which I saw Earth's suffering, and I could not act. That is a special torment for one like Me. It paused. *Everyone here is concerned for both of you, and also for our future. We have much to contemplate. It seems I have much more to learn from the Minds there.*

Her joy quickly subsided. She was free to go. She was once again linked to the Wanderer, yet dissatisfaction and disappointment still gnawed at her. She thought of Home, wondering if the cometdwellers would welcome links with Earth.

—What do you want, then?— Daiya asked. —It seems that you don't know—

—To go back—

—You can, yet that doesn't seem to please you—

Lydee tugged at her silver sleeve. —I want to forget—

Reiho raised an eyebrow.

"I want to forget," she repeated with her voice. "I don't want to remember that we're only objects for cybernetic Minds to use for some purpose of Their own. Homesmind calls me Its eye. It might better have called me one of Its cells. A body has millions of cells that die all the time, but the brain needn't concern itself with them as long as new ones are created.

Homesmind manipulated me to get me here, and used Reiho as well, and the Mindcores here have let hundreds of people die. Have you forgotten them?"

—They had Their reasons— Daiya responded.

"They gave us an explanation. They might have lied. Anyway, what sort of reasoning is that? Let some die so that others don't. It's their own purposes that concern Them, not ours. The Minds here want to live and grow stronger, and Homesmind wants to learn from Them. They have no feelings for us."

We are your servants, Homesmind said.

"You are our master. We couldn't even live on the Wanderer without You or something like You."

I am your creation, your child.

"That was long ago. You rule us now, and the Minds of Earth have surpassed even You. They've used You as You've used us. They hid Themselves and then acted too late."

—Lydee— Daiya leaned forward. —It's not the fault of the Minds that those things happened. Should They have forced Their will on us from the beginning? They might have, you know, but They left us free. I mourn those who died and wish that they could be restored, but at least they had the choice of living with truth or fleeing this world, and now others, the separate selves, the ones like you, will be able to live—

"I've done what I was sent here to do. You can't ask more of me."

—No, I can't— Daiya jabbed at the fire with a stick. "What are you going to do, Reiho?" Lydee was afraid that she already knew.

—I'll stay, at least for a while. I'll need another shuttle, and some tools— He turned toward Daiya. Lydee realized that he was again seeing the woman as the girl he had once known, and himself as the boy who had died years earlier.

—You are yourself again— Daiya thought. —You are the Reiho I knew before—

—Somehow I am. Not literally, but in some sense. All that was in him is in me, and I can accept it. Maybe that's why I've healed, because I accept him, and myself—

Daiya touched his arm.

—It's strange, isn't it?— Reiho continued. —I want to stay in the place I feared— He was no longer conscious of Lydee as Daiya drew his mind closer to hers.

Lydee rose and stomped away from the fire. She sat down again on the hillside in the darkness. Even her mentor was abandoning her now; Homesmind would have one eye on Earth. It did not matter. Her old friends on the Wanderer would help her forget.

A light fluttered across the meadow; Marellon was walking toward her with a torch. As he came up to her, he smothered the flame with his mind; darkness cloaked them as the torch sputtered out.

He sat next to her without speaking, his mind silent.

Daiya and Reiho were still communing by the fire and Lydee thought she heard Marellon sigh. The black clouds above them parted, revealing the moon's crescent and the comet's tail.

"Your wall is up," the boy said.

"I must get used to that. I'm going back to a place where one's wall is always up."

"So you're going back."

"Yes."

"Your love is so weak, Lydee."

"It isn't true. I'll always care for you in some way."

"In some way," he said mockingly. "I suppose your world's Mind will call up images of me for you, and that will be enough." She felt a pang; she had known she would disappoint him.

She turned toward him. "You could come with me, Marellon. No one would mind. Homesmind could teach you anything you wish to know. You might find life there easier and more pleasant than you think."

"No, Lydee. You don't really want me there—you're only trying to make yourself feel better about leaving. You think you should offer the invitation, that's all."

"That isn't true. I do want you to come—you must believe that."

"You would begin to compare me with those you know, and you'd see me as primitive, the way you once did. You would come to scorn me. Better to remember me as you see me now."

"Your love is as weak as mine," she burst out. "You want to keep me on your world, but you won't come to mine."

"Love doesn't have the same meaning for your people. That would divide us eventually."

He was right about that, she thought. Her people would not tear at one another over love. "I'm sorry I can't stay," she whispered.

"You're free to go. I can't hold you. Love isn't enough for either of us. We would have had to share something more—the same feeling about life and what we should do with it. A clean break is better."

"What will you do?" she asked.

"I'll stay here for a while. But some are already thinking of leaving for other villages so that those people can see that what's happened here may not be so fearful as they think. We've passed through our ordeal and can help them struggle through theirs. It might help if a few of us live among them." He paused. "I don't know if I can stay in a place where everything would only remind me of you."

"You'll soon be past that. Such intense feelings can't last for long." Her words were sensible, yet they seemed cold even to her, and false.

She stood up. "I must go. It's foolish to wait. I'll say farewell to you now."

"But you haven't said your farewells to Luret, or to Nenla and Kal, or anyone else. They'll be disappointed."

"Say them for me. I think it's better if I leave quickly. Supplies and another ship will have to be sent here, and I—" She swallowed, unable to endure the thought of long-drawn-out goodbyes. The kindly Nenla and Kal would no doubt prevail upon her to stay one more night; Luret would grieve at losing a friend. It would be simpler to spare them that, she told herself, knowing that it would also be easier for her.

"Go, then," Marellon said as he rose. "I can always try to believe that if you had stayed a little longer, I might have changed your mind."

She pulled at her finger, removing the ring her friends had given to her. "You may have this," she said. "It was a gift to me, but I want you to have it. The stone is blue, like Earth's oceans."

Marellon lashed out suddenly, knocking the ring from her hand; the wall around his thoughts buckled. —Why would I want that?— he thought. She backed away, shielding herself from his anger. "You want to forget," he said in a low voice. "I must forget, too. I won't carry your memory with me in the shape of that bauble." He turned away and strode down the hill.

—Marellon— she called out with her mind.
—Don't leave in anger—

He walked on, his shield up.

—Marellon—

She waited. He moved on across the meadow, silvered by the light of the moon and comet. At last she heard his thoughts: —Good-bye, Lydee—

—Good-bye—

She knelt, slapping the ground with one hand. A gleam caught her eye; her hand closed around the ring. She continued to watch Marellon until the clouds covered the moon and comet, hiding him from her sight.

15

The Wanderer had traveled closer to the sun along the comet's parabolic path, and the solar fire had swelled until all of space seemed filled with a bright, yellow light marred only by the mottling of sunspots. Flares arched from the fiery surface as the solar storms raged, leaping out toward the intruding comet before falling back, recaptured by the sun's gravity.

Most of the cometdwellers stayed below, inside their roots. Lydee was one of the few who ventured out, hovering near the uppermost limbs of the trees, safe behind the comet's protective energy field, her shuttle's dome darkened so that she could gaze at the heavenly fire. Homesmind, near as It was to the sun, had kept at a safe distance, and yet at times Lydee could imagine the sun roiling up and making a cinder of the thief that was stealing its light.

She traveled up through the trees to view the sun on several occasions, as if the light of the sun's atomic furnace could somehow illuminate the dark corridors inside her. Once, she knew, humankind had seen the star as an unchanging, eternal presence, but it, like the tiny creatures basking in its rays, was being transformed. Its atoms of hydrogen would combine in the violence of atomic fusion to form new elements until, billions of years later, the sun began to die. No human eyes were likely to see its death, and darkness would triumph.

As the comet fled, beginning its outward journey, the sun shrank until it was once again a baleful, but more distant, eye, gazing unwinkingly at the children who could now escape it.

Tila had proposed a game in one of the mazes, and the others had quickly agreed. Lydee had managed to find her way through the maze first. It was her turn now to design a new maze. She offered her turn to Jerod while Tila, Nara, and Pilo returned to the maze's center to wait for the boy to set up a new pattern.

The mirrored walls of the maze slid along the floor, shaping another maze as Jerod designed his labyrinth, frowning while he directed Homesmind through his link. "There," he said. "They'll have a hard time finding their way through that." The bald boy stretched out on the grassy carpet bordering the maze. "You used to like mazes."

Lydee shrugged. While searching for a way through Tila's maze, she had repressed an impulse to touch the girl's mind and read her pattern. She had found her way out alone as an infinite number of her reflected images scurried through the labyrinth with her. She had remained locked within herself, as had all of the cometdwellers since viewing Homesmind's reconstruction of what had happened on Earth.

Little had changed. The cometdwellers seemed so anxious to prove it that their normal activities were pursued with a frantic desperation. Homesmind had Its link with Earth's Minds. If Reiho wanted to dwell among primitives and guide them, that was his affair; he would tire of his Earthwoman soon enough. Etey and her friends might speak of change, even of developing their mindpowers, but if they pushed too hard, others would simply have to build a new home and leave Etey to this one.

Lydee had listened to such talk. She herself had been forgiven; she was still a child and had suffered unspeakable things. It was natural for her to feel a little concern for the planet that had given her life, but in time she would put it behind her.

Jerod nudged her with one elbow. "You're always so silent now, Lydee."

She glanced at him. His smile, as usual, warned her not to talk of anything too serious or intense. Jerod guarded himself now, as if determined not to lapse into overly emotional displays. "Words don't seem enough after you've touched others' thoughts." At least she could say that to him. Tila, Nara, and Pilo always changed the subject whenever she alluded to Earth.

"I understand."

She wondered if he did. Her friends had tried so hard to make her feel welcome during the past months that she had nearly felt smothered by their solicitude. Their courtesy and concern were only another wall between her and them.

The comet had already passed Earth's orbit on its outward journey; the planet would soon be only a tiny blue orb. "Once," she said slowly, "you told me that you would go to Earth with me."

Jerod's blue eyes widened; his smile faded for a moment. "Oh, I suppose I meant it then. I don't imagine I could go now, really I couldn't." He was stressing his words a bit too much. "It's not a place for people like us—so uncomfortable. I wouldn't get along at all—I'd be completely incompetent. I'm sure I'd be of no use to anyone and would get into all sorts of trouble." He grinned uneasily. "Anyway, I prefer being with you and my other friends here. We'll build a new home and maybe we'll leave this system. I'd like that. A lot of people want to build a new home now. I suppose they'll have their own ideas about how it's to be, but that can't be helped. Maybe we should seed two comets—one for the old and one for the young. You won't think about Earth once you're there."

Jerod had an arch tone in his voice; he was babbling again, as he often seemed to do. She gazed into his eyes intently. He stared back blankly, then suddenly looked away.

"The people of Earth didn't just suffer for themselves," she said softly. "They believed our worlds would grow closer, but the distance between us is as great. What a cruel joke Reiho's work is after all. What are the Earthpeople going to think when they learn how few here care?"

Jerod's eyes narrowed. For a moment, she almost believed that he was trying to reach out to her with his mind, but that had to be an illusion.

"They're being helped," he replied. "They have what they need. If Homesmind insists on staying in this system, then those who agree with It will stay and the rest will go. Anyway, you returned—you didn't stay behind. So you must feel the same way we do."

His words had touched her guilt. She rested her arms on her knees. "At first, I wanted to forget, but I can't. Then I thought that others would do what I couldn't do, but that won't happen. And I told myself I might be needed here, but no one is, really."

Jerod's head drooped, as if so much frank conversation had exhausted him. When he looked up again, his eyes seemed glazed. "Well, *we* need you. We simply didn't have as much fun while you were away—we're so used to being a pentagram rather than a rectangle. Your absence really did affect our interactions, you know." He waved a hand toward the maze. "Look—Pilo's the first."

The dark-haired boy hurried out of the maze. "Very clever, Jerod. But I think I can design one you won't have an easy time in."

Lydee forced herself to smile.

After seeing her friends to their dwellings, she returned to her boat. A young woman on a neighboring sailboat waved at Lydee, who returned the greeting before going below deck. Her boat swayed gently as the lake lapped softly at its hull; she heard a musical laugh and then the sound of a flute over the chatter on the boat berthed next to hers.

The people living on the lake had tolerated Lydee, asking nothing about her time on Earth. Their demands were few. She was always invited to join them in their party, a never-ending affair which died down only long enough for the participants to sleep or go sailing or visit other friends, yet no one seemed to mind when she kept to herself. One of the women often went sailing with her, but Lydee could not recall her acquaintance ever discussing anything except boats.

She took out a bottle of wine and went topside again. A few white sails skimmed over the water in the distance; the party had moved on to another dock, where the celebrants were boarding a larger boat. She sprawled on the deck in the hazy, yellow light, gulped from her bottle, then propped her head against a cushion.

She thought of her old cave, which she had abandoned. She had not wanted to stay there alone; the cave reminded her of Reiho, and that inevitably led to thoughts of Earth. Homesmind had offered her a new mentor, but she had refused, thinking that she now knew as much about life as any mentor could teach her. Homesmind had understood. She rarely spoke to It now.

What was life for? What was it supposed to be? It had become a mistake on Earth, but that was beginning to change. What was it here? Perhaps it was another kind of mistake, one which could not be seen so easily.

She stretched out, covering her eyes with one arm. The light was warm; the taste of the dry, fruited wine lingered in her mouth. A breeze from the shore carried the clean, leafy scent of trees. She would gather sensations, treasuring those most pleasurable; maybe she needed no other purpose.

The boat creaked slightly as someone boarded. She lay still, knowing that the visitor would go to another boat after realizing that Lydee did not want to be disturbed.

"Lydee?"

She sat up, turning toward the stern.

"Greetings," Genlai said. The woman's blue eyes, as usual, were dreamy and unfocused, but her hands moved nervously as she pulled at a white band of clothing, pressed her fingertips together, then let her arms fall to her sides, making fists. "I am saying my farewells." Her voice was so low that Lydee could barely hear her.

"You've said them so many times," Lydee responded in gentle tones so that the woman would not think she was being mocked.

"I think this time is the last." Genlai's voice shook on the last word.

"But why?" Lydee asked. Genlai was silent. "I don't want to probe, but I always thought that boredom and fatigue had driven you to have such a desire. You can now choose to do something new, if you want to."

"Yes. You have seen to that." Genlai's tone was still gentle, but her hands were clenched so tightly that her knuckles were white. "Things may change. It frightens me. A few speak of links with Earth while Homesmind is entranced with that old world's Mindcores. That sort of knowledge brought death to many there, and it may do the same here in time. I can't bear to live to see it."

Lydee had a sudden urge to grab the woman and shake her, but that would only frighten her away. She held out a hand. "You mustn't feel that way. I didn't come back here to watch people die because of what has happened."

"Yet even you are content to leave Earth to others—you, who were born there. Others feel as I do. We'll say our farewells and depart. Homesmind will shape us our last dreams. My death will be a peaceful and pleasant one."

"Don't speak of pleasant deaths to me, Genlai. I've seen too much death. Everything that is you will be gone, torn from this world, nonexistent. Homesmind may give you a dream, and recycle your corpse, and preserve a record of your life, but you'll no longer *be*. That can't be better than living." She had spoken too harshly; Genlai had backed away, as if ready to leap from the boat. "The Earthfolk are willing to reach out to us, even though their lives will change much more than ours."

"They are used to hard lives. I'm not." Genlai covered her eyes for a moment, then jumped from the boat before Lydee could stop her, splashing through the water to the shore.

Lydee thumbed her belt and flew toward the sand, landing in front of the woman and blocking her way. "Listen to me." Genlai shrank back, holding up a hand. "Go to another world if you want, seed a new home. Do anything, but don't die." Genlai stared passively at Lydee. "I'm responsible for this," Lydee con-

tinued. "I can bear it if people run away, or even reject
the possibility of ties with Earth, but not their deaths.
You can't leave me with that burden."

"We're free to do as we like."

"No, we're not. That's another thing I've found out."

"You ran away from Earth."

"I might have been wrong." Lydee paused, struggling for words. "You came to see me because you're
still uncertain. You really don't want to say farewells—
you're just afraid. I was afraid, too. I could have died
many times on Earth." She took the woman's hand,
helping her onto the sand, then kept her grip, afraid
that Genlai might flee.

"I've never felt a fear like this." She leaned against
Lydee. "I wish things could be as they were."

"I do, too. But they can't."

"Walk with me, child. You are the only one who
has asked me to live." They made their way along the
beach as people on docks and boats called out greetings
in musical voices.

As Lydee walked back to her dock, she wondered if
she had aided Genlai at all. The woman had promised
to speak to her other unhappy friends, and Homesmind
would not allow her to die in this uncertainty, but her
fear would not disappear soon. Genlai had a new weapon,
if she chose to use it; she could open her link and turn
her mind against itself.

As she stepped onto the dock, she saw that Etey was

waiting on her boat. "How nice to see you," Lydee said without meaning it as she stepped aboard and sat down on a cushion.

—We can mindspeak, if you prefer—

Lydee raised her head.

"Oh, yes," Etey continued aloud. "I have been practicing with a couple of my more daring friends. I'm afraid it hasn't made me very popular. It's been difficult. I worried that too many feelings I might be unaware of would come out, that I wouldn't be able to deal with them. Well, I needn't have worried. It seems I've lived too long to feel anything very intensely, except perhaps for curiosity." She sounded almost disappointed at lacking emotional depths.

"You're fortunate, then. Many can still feel fear." Lydee sighed. "I'd rather not mindspeak right now."

"We might have used your help."

"For what?"

"To contribute your ideas on what we should do for Earth."

"We're already helping."

"Oh, we send Reiho what he needs. But that isn't enough, Lydee. What are we to do when or if the Earthdwellers want more contact with us? What will it do to them when they realize we don't really care?"

Lydee did not reply.

"Oh, well. We are all in shock, so to speak, but that always passes."

Lydee frowned. "What an odd way to put it."

"It's obvious. Do you think only Earth has discovered how insignificant it is? Do you believe that it's the only culture that must renew itself? So must we. If we reject what has happened and don't change, we'll either rot or tear ourselves apart. In time, we may meet something else that doesn't fit into our tidy lives, and then we may be destroyed one way or another. We're not the only beings in the universe, you know."

"I suppose Homesmind sent you. It can speak for Itself."

"But then you might not have listened. No, I came by myself. Homesmind has other things to concern It now." Etey leaned back. "It knows what It has to do—exchange Its thoughts and ideas with Its cybernetic sisters on Earth. It's already learning how to open more of our links. And if all of that means exiling those who want to keep things as they are, then that is what It will do. Of course, it won't seem like an expulsion. Those leaving this world will choose to do so. The result will be the same."

"And some will choose to die."

"Perhaps. Beings die and new beings are born."

"My friends want to seed a new world."

Etey shrugged. "Usually it happens when younger people want to explore or try something new and wish to rid themselves of the weight of the old. Now it will happen because many want to escape the new." She stood up and began to pace along the deck. "I've been toying with various possibilities. Some of our children might spend time on Earth, and theirs might visit here. That probably won't happen right away, but we have time." She turned and leaned against the cabin. "At least we do. Earthpeople have such short lives. Perhaps they should be extended. We'll have to be very cautious—hasty decisions could be damaging. We can't simply treat them as subjects, and they might not regard what we have to offer as a benefit. Reiho worries about the possible destruction of what is worthwhile in their culture, as you know. Or maybe you don't, since you haven't bothered to communicate with him."

Lydee's shoulders sagged. "I thought it was over. I thought I could come back here and let others deal with Earth. I don't know what to do, Etey."

Etey crossed the deck and climbed off the boat. "I'll be going to Earth soon." Lydee gazed at her in surprise. "Someone else must put in an appearance. Reiho would like to have me there, and Daiya says she will welcome me this time. Good-bye, Lydee." She strode down the dock without looking back.

Lydee's friends had joined the ongoing party by the lake, wandering from boat to boat until they arrived at her dock. Globes of light floated near the water, illuminating Lydee's boat as the group clambered on board. The light overhead had been dimmed and the people around the lake were enjoying the darkness of night.

Lydee settled the four young people on cushions,

summoned food and drink, and let them chatter. Nara and Tila described a butterfly-filled garden they planned to tend together while Pilo offered a few suggestions and Jerod mentioned a design of stones he might embed in the garden's paths.

During a lull in the conversation, Lydee cleared her throat. "The lattices," Tila murmured. "Lydee can design the lattices, maybe weave the vines."

Lydee said, "I'm thinking of going back to Earth."

Jerod was still. Nara's mouth opened slightly; Tila's arm froze as she was about to pour more wine. Pilo drew up his legs slowly, wrapping his arms around them.

"Reiho's old mentor is going, and I think she'll be happy to take me with her." She waited, expecting them either to change the subject or to make up reasons for leaving early. "I had to tell you. You would have found out soon enough."

Jerod said, "I'm not surprised."

"Well, I am," Nara said quietly.

"I suppose you think I'm foolish to consider it," Lydee said.

Jerod shook his head. "No. May I speak honestly?" He looked around shyly at the others. "When you first came back, you tried to act as though you hadn't really changed, but I knew that couldn't be after what you went through. I wanted to reach out to you, but I was afraid to do it. You might have misunderstood. It seemed that you wanted us to be as we were and yet you seemed unhappy with that. In a way, I was almost disappointed that you didn't ask more of us." The boy seemed flustered; he rubbed at his jaw, then folded his arms. "When I saw that you were really going to stay, I wondered what it meant—perhaps that you were rejecting Earth and wanted us to do the same. But it isn't that, is it?"

Lydee was silent.

"You're running away. Somehow Earth must have opened up parts of yourself you didn't want to know, so you retreated, like a child clinging to the nursery or to a mentor. I think you must have grown to love that world, but there was too much of this one in you to let you admit it. And you didn't want the responsibility of trying to work with them, or even with us, and maybe making a mistake. You were afraid." He took a deep breath. "Well, I'm afraid, too. That talk of seeding another comet—it would just be running away." He shaded his eyes, as if ashamed of having said so much.

Nara stood up and lurched toward the dock. Pilo reached for her, pulling her down. The white-haired girl shivered.

"Well," Tila said nervously.

"Well," Lydee said.

"I suppose," Tila murmured, "you must be used to that sort of frankness after sharing your thoughts with others." She pulled at her long, brown hair. "Fears should be kept to oneself, shouldn't they?" She turned toward Jerod apprehensively.

"No, they shouldn't," he said abruptly. "They fester."

"It wasn't just fear we shared," Lydee responded, "or anger or hatred. There was friendship and love, too. A girl there was my friend, and I cared for a boy." At last she had admitted that to them openly. "They read my thoughts and knew what I was inside, and yet they cared for me anyway."

"I see," Pilo said. "Maybe they are your true friends, then."

"Maybe they are. I came to love the boy, in my own way. Not that it matters now. I was ashamed of it when I came back."

"It must be hard to share thoughts so readily," Tila said.

"It is. Even the Earthfolk can't always do it easily. One has to be honest, even about hiding one's thoughts. They always know when you're hiding them, you see. Here, we pretend we don't know."

"It frightens me," Jerod said. "Some on this comet are already trying to share their thoughts and use their powers. Sometimes I fear that if others saw my mind as it really is, they would hate me, and at other times I'm afraid I might lash out at them."

"We've lived without such powers all this time," Nara said, "and our lives have been good."

"Homesmind has waited for this," Lydee said. "It knew we would have to communicate with Earth again, It knew I would have to go back, and I suppose It prepared me for the journey all my life somehow. We grew up together, so It must have prepared you, too. You may be capable of more than you realize." She sighed. "I must go back, and eventually, others may follow."

"I wish you wouldn't go," Pilo whispered.

"I have to."

"You could help us. We could consider these matters together."

"You can still speak to me through Homesmind. You might even want to come to Earth sometime."

Jerod shook his head. "Not right away. Maybe not ever." His voice had resumed its old, steady tone. He raised his glass. "We should celebrate. You mustn't return without happy memories."

She reached for his hand and held it tightly.

"Go on," Etey said. "I need some time to prepare myself."

Lydee nodded, sensing Etey's apprehension. She climbed out of the shuttle and walked by the side of a ditch toward the village. The air was warm; the grass on the meadow had brown and yellow patches among the green.

Homesmind had prepared her for what she would

find. The huts on the village's periphery were already crumbling; several had holes in their roofs. The path she was following through the town was green with weeds, while briars and unpruned flowers had taken over gardens. She had not thought so much could change in only a year.

As she came nearer to the public space, she noticed more order; here the paths had been kept clean and the gardens tended. Chickens clucked as she passed; she sensed the murmur of minds. But the village's Net was now only thin threads.

Cerwen, Leito, and a few other Merging Selves sat in the open space communing with Reiho. Cerwen looked up, smiling when he saw her; Leito held up a hand. Lydee touched their minds gently. They were speaking with Earth's Minds, learning more of the past; their thoughts seemed sharper and more angular.

—There is sorrow in what we have lost— Cerwen said as he caught her thoughts. —But we have found some joy in what we are learning. Welcome back, child—

She withdrew and turned to greet Nenla and Kal as they entered the public space. The red-haired woman hurried toward her. —We've been waiting for you— Nenla said.

—I didn't realize how few of you were left— Her mindspeech seemed awkward; she would have to get used to it all over again. —You've lost your village after all—

—It will change. More children will be brought here, and the village will grow— Nenla's words were tinged with doubt. —We have already had one village ask us to accept a child born as a separate self, and others are sure to follow—

—But why did so many leave?—

—It's best that most live elsewhere— Kal replied, —to help others through this period. But I know that there were also many who wanted to leave a place that reminded them of the sorrows they once felt. They are part of another Net now—

Lydee thought of Marellon and then hid behind her wall.

—My brother is far from here— Nenla said; she had touched the memory before Lydee could hide it. —He went with Luret and Wiland to a village far to the south. I hope he has found some happiness there—

—Don't you know? You can speak to him, can't you?— The Minds, she knew, could now link one village to another without the aid of Merging Selves.

—I could. But he has not spoken to me or reached out to us, and I have come to think he needs his time of forgetfulness. Luret and Wiland are now partners. Perhaps Marellon has found someone by now—

Lydee stared at her feet, hiding her thoughts.

—Did you think he would wait when he believed

you would not return? A love like that must be put aside, or it poisons. You may call to him if you wish— Nenla thought more kindly. —You have the power. You might have spoken to him from the comet, but you did not, I see—

—I don't want to cause him more pain—

Kal patted her shoulder. —Rejoice with us— the dark-haired man said. —At last we'll have another child— He touched his partner's belly. Lydee tried to smile.

Reiho stood up, leaving the Merging Selves to their thoughts. His hair was shaggier, his brown tunic frayed at the edges; he looked like another villager. He went to her and gripped her by the shoulders.

—I'm glad you came back, Lydee—

—I suppose it is my home, after all—

—Are you going to stay?—

—Yes, I suppose I shall. But I thought there would be more for me to do here. It doesn't seem that you really need me—

Reiho shook his head. —It may seem peaceful now, but that's going to change. Tomorrow, I'll be fetching a child from the south, and there will soon be others, more solitaries. At least this time the parents welcomed the child's birth, for they think the baby will be happy here— His mood darkened. —I know that others have been killed. We learned of that too late before we could stop it, though we probably couldn't have prevented it without force and might have made things worse if we had tried. There are still many who can't accept the new way—

—There must be something you can do—

—What?— The word pricked her. —We'll have enough to do helping those who ask for our aid. We can't save everyone. That was a hard thing for me to learn—

She put a hand to her head, feeling dizzy. Reiho led her toward a hut as Nenla and Kal joined the Merging Selves, and seated her on a bench near a rosebush. "You're not used to mindspeaking, I see."

"I spent a year without it." He sat down next to her. "I longed to reach out sometimes, but knew I would only drive others away if I tried. Now I'm here, and I find that there are always walls. I could never become a Merging Self, I'm sure."

"Nor could I." He glanced at the old people. "They fall more often into their private thoughts now. I wonder if that's how it will be for all Merging Selves."

"Reiho, I'm worried. So many on the Wanderer want nothing to do with all this."

"I know."

"Genlai wanted to die. She meant it this time." She paused. "I suppose that's what made me decide to return, in a way. I had to show her and the others who felt as she did that I wasn't running away, too. At least now she'll wait."

He took her hand. "I must tell you something to cheer you. Harel and Silla have a child at last. Silla gave birth yesterday." He winced at the mention of that subject.

"A normal child?"

"A solitary."

"Then it will be the first child to live here. I should go visit them."

"I wouldn't advise it. Daiya and Harel told me to keep up my wall and sent me away from the hut when it started. It's still hard to think of it—having children that way. Daiya chides me because I can't give her one, so her sister's baby may fill that need for her."

"I'll have to get used to it, so I may as well face it." She shuddered as she rose. "I'll go to them. Etey is waiting in the shuttle—I'm sure she'll want to see you now."

Silla was outside her hut, apparently over the rigors of birth. She sat by her garden holding the child, a squirming, bald creature clad only in a piece of cloth around its bottom. Lydee saw that Silla had bared her breasts; the baby was suckling. She covered her mouth, shielding her mind until her nausea passed.

"Greetings, Silla."

The woman looked up. —You may mindspeak with me. I no longer fear your thoughts—

Lydee shook her head. "I must get used to it again."

Silla's lip curled. "You mean you must get used to this, and hide your feelings." She gestured at a bare breast. "You skydwellers are squeamish."

The child gurgled, gazing up at Lydee with Harel's blue eyes. A pale rivulet trickled to its chin; it smelled of urine. She wrinkled her nose, trying to block the odor.

"She's a girl," Silla continued. "A solitary. She is Anra SillaHarel. Daiya chose the name, though I had hoped our mother's name would go to a normal child."

"But you know that she won't remain that way. When she has her implant, her powers will be like yours."

"She'll have a crutch, you mean, like a cripple. I have tried to accept her, but I reach out and she can't even sense my thoughts. It's hard to form a bond. I see why it's best that such children be with others like themselves." Silla pulled her shirt down, then rubbed the child's back. "Daiya tells me that the world will come to accept such separate selves and will commune freely with them, but I'm not so sure. Reiho hopes for others to come here from the sky, but when I touch his thoughts, I see his doubts."

"Some will come here eventually."

"I don't think they should. Let Reiho or your world's Mind teach the people here how to give such children their crutches. Then you can go back to your own world."

"But we want these children to be part of both worlds."

"They'll never be that. I think that they'll always be separate both from this world and from yours. They will be like you, Lydee."

It was the first time Silla had used her name. "And what am I like?"

"You look for a purpose. You try to fill the empty spot I see inside you. Your mind has sharp edges and is filled with strange thoughts. You divide time into segments and see a line stretching from one place to another instead of an eternal cycle. You separate yourself from this world with machines and devices, and think we will come to do the same."

"I might become more like you."

"But you'll never be one of us, and you aren't a true skydweller, either. You're an exile." Silla shrugged. "Well, I have a child, poor creature that she is, and there will be others. Maybe they won't be like this one, though if they are, we'll send them here." She rested the child's head on her shoulder. "Harel and I will soon go to another village, and leave Anra here." There was a note of triumph in her voice; Daiya, too, would be left behind. "That will be best. She'll be with those like her."

Daiya and Harel were walking toward them along the path, carrying buckets of water. They smiled when they saw Lydee, but showed no surprise; they had already known she was there.

Silla stood up. "Take her." She thrust the baby at Lydee, who held Anra gingerly, uncertain about what to do with her. The baby wailed; her covering felt damp. Lydee made a face; Anra screamed. Daiya laughed as she set down her bucket.

"I have much to learn," Lydee said, handing the child back to Silla. "I can't even hold her without making her cry."

Harel went to Silla and took his daughter from her. "You'll learn," Daiya said. "The Merging Selves have raised many children and they'll show you what to do." A wistful look passed over her face as she gazed at the baby.

"You don't need me for that. Our teachers and guides should come here—they know more than I do."

"You will learn."

Harel crooned to Anra, rocking her gently in his arms. Daiya beckoned to Lydee; they began to stroll along the path toward another hut. "Anra will come to see us as her parents rather than Silla and Harel," Daiya said.

I shouldn't have come back, Lydee thought to herself, already feeling useless as she followed her sister into the hut.

Lydee sat on the hill. Daiya's old hut had become only a heap of bricks; vines had begun to sprout along the remaining wall.

In the distance, Daiya was walking along the river-bank with Etey. At least Daiya had found some contentment; she had been sharing a hut with Reiho. Her feelings for him might be feeble compared to what she had once felt for Harel, but Reiho too was still learning how to share himself. He would have no time to concern himself with Lydee.

She could go back to the comet; her friends there would understand. Earth would be a series of images in Homesmind's thoughts. Here, she was in the way, someone to be given useless tasks to keep her busy. She had felt the pity of the remaining villagers.

The sun was setting. Those tilling the fields put down their tools and walked toward the huts. Perhaps she should rebuild Daiya's old house and live outside the village as her sister had.

She heard a faint hum, and looked up. Reiho was returning from the south, where he had gone that morning to bring back a child. His shuttle floated over the hill, dipped toward the meadow, and landed near the fields. The door opened. Reiho got out; a pair of hands handed him a small bundle. A parent, or someone else willing to help with the children, must have returned with him. She turned back toward the river.

—Lydee—

The thought was faint, but clear. She raised her head, sensing a familiar mind. Three people were standing next to the shuttle; as she watched, they lifted themselves and began to fly toward her. She clasped her hands together.

—Marellon— she called out.

He soared, dived, then alighted in front of her as Luret and Wiland landed next to him. Their minds sang as they ran to her; Luret and Marellon embraced her as Wiland stood to one side.

—Reiho told us you'd come back— Luret said. —He spoke to us through the Minds and stopped for us on the way back. We had to come when we found out you were here—

Lydee swallowed, unable to mindspeak. She had not told Reiho to do that.

/No/ a voice said inside her. /But We did. We can show kindness, you see/ She wondered if it was kindness after all; Marellon might have come only to say another farewell to her.

Luret put up her wall, then led Wiland a short distance down the hill, leaving Marellon alone with Lydee.

"I thought you might have found a partner by now," she said as the boy sat down.

"No. I want no partner. Whenever I went to another, I saw you, and she would sense that, and I would touch a body without touching a mind. That is worse than no love at all." He paused. —Do we need that clumsy talk—

—No— She reached for his hand. There were hollows in his cheeks; his face was leaner, more like a man's. —I may give you sorrow, Marellon. I have been thinking of leaving again—

—But this time I see that you're fighting against it—

—You wouldn't have children with me. I know Earthfolk set great store by that—

—I do not want them with another. There are enough on Earth who will have them—

—I would have to watch you age—

—You can always see me as you want to see me with your thoughts. My mind will be the same. And even when I'm gone, my image can speak to you, for I believe the Minds under the mountains preserve the souls of the dead—

He was wrong. The Minds held only their memories, as Homesmind did, not actual patterns of those who had once lived; she was sure of that. It could not be anything more; she wished that she could believe it were.

—Call it what you will— Marellon thought. —We have always believed that the dead live on, and it's possible that the Minds gather their souls. I've felt the warmth of human thoughts mingled with the cold flames of those Minds. We don't yet know all that the Minds can do. I've spoken to Them often, and through Them to your Homesmind. I have seen distant stars and other worlds. I have viewed the past and have seen what we have lost, and also how small we are— Marellon's mind seemed lonelier than she remembered, but the bitterness and anger she had once sensed in him were gone.

—I'm happy you're here— she said, though he had sensed that. —But there is nothing for me to do. I seem to be useless wherever I go—

—But you could come with us when we leave again. Would you be willing to do that?—

She drew back. —Then you aren't staying here, in the village?—

—We came to see if you would journey with us, Lydee. It isn't wise to wait until others come to us. We must reach out more, perhaps to villages in other parts of Earth. We want to travel from village to village and mindspeak with those who still shrink from what has happened. It's hard for some to speak with the Minds, and many fear the power those Minds can give them. If they see you, they may stop fearing you and your ways, and with us as your companions, they'll know that friendship with you and other skydwellers is possible. That is something you could do—

—It could be dangerous—

—Of course. Some may chase us away or strike out. Others may wall themselves in. We can't force ourselves on anyone, but some may learn to accept us. And we should try to save those who still die, the separate selves—

—But I can't live as you do. I'll need supplies—

—You'll have your vessel. That would be easier than traveling on foot or on horseback. With the vessel, we'll also be able to offer them gifts, and that may help us—

—But when they see the tools I have— she objected, —they might only feel primitive and inferior—

Marellon laughed. —When they see that you require such things, they'll feel superior to you. It's just as well. That way, they'll keep their pride—

That sort of life, she saw, would be something they could share, though to have it they would have to give up the lives they might have had. She would lose her old world, but Marellon would also be a wanderer without his own hut and village. She sighed. Love, apparently, required such sacrifices.

He looked down. —Will you come— he asked, —or are you trying to find another objection?—

—I'll go with you, Marellon— Her link glowed inside her for a moment; Homesmind was content.

—Look— He gestured at the village. Flowers suddenly blossomed around the huts, which were abruptly transformed, becoming crystal structures with twinkling facets. The streets, now wider, were alive with people, some clothed in robes or tunics, others wearing silver lifesuits. Shuttles sat at the edges of the fields and near a tree-lined park; overhead, the comet appeared, lighting the sky. A beam of light shot up from the village, pointing to the heavens as the people below called out to the universe, seeking other intelligences. Marellon, with the power of the Minds, was showing her his vision of how Earth was to be.

The images faded; the shabby village reappeared.

—Perhaps— she said, hoping.

About the Author

Pamela Sargent has been called "one of the leaders in a new generation of novelists" by writer Gregory Benford and "an able and unusual storyteller" by novelist Michael Bishop. Her novels include CLONED LIVES, THE SUDDEN STAR, WATCHSTAR, THE GOLDEN SPACE, and THE ALIEN UPSTAIRS. She is also the author of a collection of short stories, STARSHADOWS, and has edited four anthologies: WOMEN OF WONDER, BIO-FUTURES, MORE WOMEN OF WONDER, and THE NEW WOMEN OF WONDER. Ms. Sargent's first novel for young people, EARTHSEED, was called "a gripping, emotion-evoking narrative" by the ALA *Booklist* in a starred review; Andre Norton praised it as a "new and striking adventure story." EYE OF THE COMET is her seventh novel and her second for young adults. She lives in upstate New York.